THE STORIES OF F. SCOTT FITZGERALD

VOLUME 5 THE LOST DECADE
AND OTHER STORIES

In Scott Fitzgerald, as in every writer of genius, there was something of the seer. He gave a name to an age – the Jazz Age – lived through that age, and saw it burn itself out. As a *New York Times* editorial stated after his death: 'He was better than he knew, for in fact and in the literary sense he invented a "generation" . . . he might have interpreted them and even guided them, as in their middle years they saw a different and nobler freedom threatened with destruction.'

F. Scott Fitzgerald was born in 1896 and educated in St Paul, Minnesota. He began writing when he was a schoolboy, and continued while at Princeton. In 1917 he left university for the army – but didn't get to France – and wrote in his spare moments. Then came *This Side of Paradise* – the first of his novels – followed by two volumes of short stories, and at last *The Great Gatsby*, which alone would assure Scott Fitzgerald's place among writers of major stature. He died in 1940.

Besides *The Great Gatsby* and *This Side of Paradise*, he wrote three other novels, *The Beautiful and Damned*, *Tender is the Night*, and *The Last Tycoon* (his last and unfinished work); and five volumes of short stories, which include *The Crack-Up*, a selection of his autobiographical pieces.

D1155615

The Stories of F. Scott Fitzgerald

Volume 5
The Lost Decade
and Other Stories

Penguin Books

PENGUIN BOOKS

Published by the Penguin Group
Penguin Books Ltd, 27 Wrights Lane, London W8 5TZ, England
Penguin Books USA Inc., 375 Hudson Street, New York, New York 10014, USA
Penguin Books Australia Ltd, Ringwood, Victoria, Australia
Penguin Books Canada Ltd, 10 Alcorn Avenue, Toronto, Ontario, Canada M4V 3B2
Penguin Books (NZ) Ltd, 182–190 Wairau Road, Auckland 10, New Zealand

Penguin Books Ltd, Registered Offices: Harmondsworth, Middlesex, England

'Basil: The Freshest Boy' first published 1928
'Josephine: A Woman with a Past' first published 1930
'Two Wrongs' first published 1930
'The Bridal Party' first published 1930
'Crazy Sunday' first published 1932
'Three Hours Between Planes' first published 1941
'The Lost Decade' first published 1939

Published by The Bodley Head in
The Bodley Head Scott Fitzgerald, Volume 6, 1963
Published in Penguin Books 1968
20 19 18 17 16 15 14 13 12

Printed in England by Clays Ltd, St Ives plc
Set in Linotype Pilgrim

Except in the United States of America, this book is sold subject
to the condition that it shall not, by way of trade or otherwise, be lent,
re-sold, hired out, or otherwise circulated without the publisher's
prior consent in any form of binding or cover other than that in
which it is published and without a similar condition including this
condition being imposed on the subsequent purchaser

Contents

Basil: The Freshest Boy

[1928]

I

It was a hidden Broadway restaurant in the dead of the night, and a brilliant and mysterious group of society people, diplomats and members of the underworld were there. A few minutes ago the sparkling wine had been flowing and a girl had been dancing gaily upon a table, but now the whole crowd were hushed and breathless. All eyes were fixed upon the masked but well-groomed man in the dress suit and opera hat who stood nonchalantly in the door.

'Don't move, please,' he said, in a well-bred, cultivated voice that had, nevertheless, a ring of steel in it. 'This thing in my hand might – go off.'

His glance roved from table to table – fell upon the malignant man higher up with his pale saturnine face, upon Heatherly, the suave secret agent from a foreign power, then rested a little longer, a little more softly perhaps, upon the table where the girl with dark hair and dark tragic eyes sat alone.

'Now that my purpose is accomplished, it might interest you to know who I am.' There was a gleam of expectation in every eye. The breast of the dark-eyed girl heaved faintly and a tiny burst of subtle French perfume rose into the air. 'I am none other than that elusive gentleman, Basil Lee, better known as the Shadow.'

Taking off his well-fitting opera hat, he bowed ironically from the waist. Then, like a flash, he turned and was gone into the night.

'You get up to New York only once a month,' Lewis Crum was saying, 'and then you have to take a master along.'

Slowly, Basil Lee's glazed eyes turned from the barns and

billboards of the Indiana countryside to the interior of the Broadway Limited. The hypnosis of the swift telegraph poles faded and Lewis Crum's stolid face took shape against the white slip-cover of the opposite bench.

'I'd just duck the master when I got to New York,' said Basil.

'Yes, you would!'

'I bet I would.'

'You try it and you'll see.'

'What do you mean saying I'll see, all the time, Lewis? What'll I see?'

His very bright dark-blue eyes were at this moment fixed upon his companion with boredom and impatience. The two had nothing in common except their age, which was fifteen, and the lifelong friendship of their fathers – which is less than nothing. Also they were bound from the same Middle-Western city for Basil's first and Lewis's second year at the same Eastern school.

But, contrary to all the best traditions, Lewis the veteran was miserable and Basil the neophyte was happy. Lewis hated school. He had grown entirely dependent on the stimulus of a hearty vital mother, and as he felt her slipping farther and farther away from him, he plunged deeper into misery and homesickness. Basil, on the other hand, had lived with such intensity on so many stories of boarding-school life that, far from being homesick, he had a glad feeling of recognition and familiarity. Indeed, it was with some sense of doing the appropriate thing, having the traditional rough-house, that he had thrown Lewis's comb off the train at Milwaukee last night for no reason at all.

To Lewis, Basil's ignorant enthusiasm was distasteful – his instinctive attempt to dampen it had contributed to the mutual irritation.

'I'll tell you what you'll see,' he said ominously. 'They'll catch you smoking and put you on bounds.'

'No, they won't, because I won't be smoking. I'll be in training for football.'

'Football! Yeah! Football!'

'Honestly, Lewis, you don't like anything, do you?'

'I don't like football. I don't like to go out and get a crack in the eye.' Lewis spoke aggressively, for his mother had canonized all his timidities as common sense. Basil's answer, made with what he considered kindly intent, was the sort of remark that creates lifelong enmities.

'You'd probably be a lot more popular in school if you played football,' he suggested patronizingly.

Lewis did not consider himself unpopular. He did not think of it in that way at all. He was astounded.

'You wait!' he cried furiously. 'They'll take all that freshness out of you.'

'Clam yourself,' said Basil, coolly plucking at the creases of his first long trousers. 'Just clam yourself.'

'I guess everybody knows you were the freshest boy at the Country Day!'

'Clam yourself,' repeated Basil, but with less assurance. 'Kindly clam yourself.'

'I guess I know what they had in the school paper about you –'

Basil's own coolness was no longer perceptible.

'If you don't clam yourself,' he said darkly, 'I'm going to throw your brushes off the train too.'

The enormity of this threat was effective. Lewis sank back in his seat, snorting and muttering, but undoubtedly calmer. His reference had been to one of the most shameful passages in his companion's life. In a periodical issued by the boys of Basil's late school there had appeared under the heading Personals:

If someone will please poison young Basil, or find some other means to stop his mouth, the school at large and myself will be much obliged.

The two boys sat there fuming wordlessly at each other. Then, resolutely, Basil tried to re-inter this unfortunate souvenir of the past. All that was behind him now. Perhaps he had been a little fresh, but he was making a new start. After a moment, the memory passed and with it the train and Lewis's dismal presence – the breath of the East came sweeping over him again with a vast nostalgia. A voice called him out of the fabled world; a man stood beside him with a hand on his sweater-clad shoulder.

'Lee!'

'Yes, sir.'

'It all depends on you now. Understand?'

'Yes, sir.'

'All right,' the coach said, 'go in and win.'

Basil tore the sweater from his stripling form and dashed out on the field. There were two minutes to play and the score was 3 to 0 for the enemy, but at the sight of young Lee, kept out of the game all year by a malicious plan of Dan Haskins, the school bully, and Weasel Weems, his toady, a thrill of hope went over the St Regis stand.

'33–12–16–22!' barked Midget Brown, the diminutive little quarterback.

It was his signal –

'Oh, gosh!' Basil spoke aloud, forgetting the late unpleasantness. 'I wish we'd get there before tomorrow.'

2

St Regis School, Eastchester,
November 18, 19—

Dear Mother:

There is not much to say today, but I thought I would write you about my allowance. All the boys have a bigger allowance than me, because there are a lot of little things I have to get, such as shoe laces, etc. School is still very nice and am having a fine time, but football is over and there is not much to do. I am going to New York this week to see a show. I do not know yet what it will be, but probably the Quacker Girl or little boy Blue as they are both very good. Dr Bacon is very nice and there's a good phycission in the village. No more now as I have to study Algebra.

Your affectionate Son,
Basil D. Lee.

As he put the letter in its envelope, a wizened little boy came into the deserted study hall where he sat and stood staring at him.

'Hello,' said Basil, frowning.

'I been looking for you,' said the little boy, slowly and judicially. 'I looked all over – up in your room and out in the gym, and they said you probably might of sneaked off in here.'

'What do you want?' Basil demanded.

'Hold your horses, Bossy.'

Basil jumped to his feet. The little boy retreated a step.

'Go on, hit me!' he chirped nervously. 'Go on, hit me, cause I'm just half your size – Bossy.'

Basil winced. 'You call me that again and I'll spank you.'

'No, you won't spank me. Brick Wales said if you ever touched any of us –'

'But I never did touch any of you.'

'Didn't you chase a lot of us one day and didn't Brick Wales –'

'Oh, what do you want?' Basil cried in desperation.

'Doctor Bacon wants you. They sent me after you and somebody said maybe you sneaked in here.'

Basil dropped his letter in his pocket and walked out – the little boy and his invective following him through the door. He traversed a long corridor, muggy with that odour best described as the smell of stale caramels that is so peculiar to boys' schools, ascended a stairs and knocked at an unexceptional but formidable door.

Doctor Bacon was at his desk. He was a handsome, redheaded Episcopal clergyman of fifty whose original real interest in boys was now tempered by the flustered cynicism which is the fate of all headmasters and settles on them like green mould. There were certain preliminaries before Basil was asked to sit down – gold-rimmed glasses had to be hoisted up from nowhere by a black cord and fixed on Basil to be sure that he was not an impostor; great masses of paper on the desk had to be shuffled through, not in search of anything but as a man nervously shuffles a pack of cards.

'I had a letter from your mother this morning – ah – Basil.' The use of his first name had come to startle Basil. No one else in school had yet called him anything but Bossy or Lee. 'She feels that your marks have been poor. I believe you have been sent here at a certain amount of – ah – sacrifice and she expects –'

Basil's spirit writhed with shame, not at his poor marks but that his financial inadequacy should be so bluntly stated. He knew that he was one of the poorest boys in a rich boys' school.

Perhaps some dormant sensibility in Doctor Bacon became aware of his discomfort; he shuffled through the papers once more and began on a new note.

'However, that was not what I sent for you about this afternoon. You applied last week for permission to go to New York on Saturday, to a matinée. Mr Davis tells me that for almost the first time since school opened you will be off bounds tomorrow.'

'Yes, sir.'

'That is not a good record. However, I would allow you to go to New York if it could be arranged. Unfortunately, no masters are available this Saturday.'

Basil's mouth dropped ajar. 'Why, I – why, Doctor Bacon, I know two parties that are going. Couldn't I go with one of them?'

Doctor Bacon ran through all his papers very quickly. 'Unfortunately, one is composed of slightly older boys and the other group made arrangements some weeks ago.'

'How about the party that's going to the *Quaker Girl* with Mr Dunn?'

'It's that party I speak of. They feel that the arrangements are complete and they have purchased seats together.'

Suddenly Basil understood. At the look in his eye Doctor Bacon went on hurriedly:

'There's perhaps one thing I can do. Of course there must be several boys in the party so that the expenses of the master can be divided up among all. If you can find two other boys who would like to make up a party, and let me have their names by five o'clock, I'll send Mr Rooney with you.'

'Thank you,' Basil said.

Doctor Bacon hesitated. Beneath the cynical incrustations of many years an instinct stirred to look into the unusual case of this boy and find out what made him the most detested boy in school. Among boys and masters there seemed to exist an extraordinary hostility towards him, and though Doctor Bacon had dealt with many sorts of schoolboy crimes, he had neither by himself nor with the aid of trusted sixth-formers been able to lay his hands on its underlying cause. It was probably no single thing, but a combination of things; it was most probably one of those intangible questions of personality. Yet he remembered that when he first saw Basil he had considered him unusually prepossessing.

He sighed. Sometimes these things worked themselves out. He wasn't one to rush in clumsily. 'Let us have a better report to send home next month, Basil.'

'Yes, sir.'

Basil ran quickly downstairs to the recreation room. It was Wednesday and most of the boys had already gone into the village of Eastchester, whither Basil, who was still on bounds, was forbidden to follow. When he looked at those still scattered about the pool tables and piano, he saw that it was going to be difficult to get anyone to go with him at all. For Basil was quite conscious that he was the most unpopular boy at school.

It had begun almost immediately. One day, less than a fortnight after he came, a crowd of the smaller boys, perhaps urged on to it, gathered suddenly around him and began calling him Bossy. Within the next week he had two fights, and both times the crowd was vehemently and eloquently with the other boy. Soon after, when he was merely shoving indiscriminately, like everyone else, to get into the dining-room, Carver, the captain of the football team, turned about and, seizing him by the back of the neck, held him and dressed him down savagely. He joined a group innocently at the piano and was told, 'Go on away. We don't want you around.'

After a month he began to realize the full extent of his unpopularity. It shocked him. One day after a particularly bitter humiliation he went up to his room and cried. He tried to keep out of the way for a while, but it didn't help. He was accused of sneaking off here and there, as if bent on a series of nefarious errands. Puzzled and wretched, he looked at his face in the glass, trying to discover there the secret of their dislike – in the expression of his eyes, his smile.

He saw now that in certain ways he had erred at the outset – he had boasted, he had been considered yellow at football, he had pointed out people's mistakes to them, he had showed off his rather extraordinary fund of general information in class. But he had tried to do better and couldn't understand his failure to atone. It must be too late. He was queered forever.

He had, indeed, become the scapegoat, the immediate villain, the sponge which absorbed all malice and irritability abroad – just as the most frightened person in a party seems to absorb all the others' fear, seems to be afraid for them all. His situation was not helped by the fact, obvious to all, that the supreme self-confidence with which he had come to St Regis in September was thoroughly broken. Boys taunted him with impunity who would not have dared raise their voices to him several months before.

This trip to New York had come to mean everything to him – surcease from the misery of his daily life as well as a glimpse into the long-waited heaven of romance. Its postponement for week after week due to his sins – he was constantly caught reading after lights, for example, driven by his wretchedness into such vicarious escapes from reality – had deepened his longing until it was a burning hunger. It was unbearable that he should not go, and he told over the short list of those whom he might get to accompany him. The possibilities were Fat Gaspar, Treadway, and Bugs Brown. A quick journey to their rooms showed that they had all availed themselves of the Wednesday permission to go into Eastchester for the afternoon.

Basil did not hesitate. He had until five o'clock and his only chance was to go after them. It was not the first time he had broken bounds, though the last attempt had ended in disaster and an extension of his confinement. In his room, he put on a heavy sweater – an overcoat was a betrayal of intent – replaced his jacket over it and hid a cap in his back pocket. Then he went downstairs and with an elaborate careless whistle struck out across the lawn for the gymnasium. Once there, he stood for a while as if looking in the windows, first the one close to the walk, then one near the corner of the building. From here he moved quickly, but not too quickly, into a grove of lilacs. Then he dashed around the corner, down a long stretch of lawn that was blind from all windows and, parting the strands of a wire fence, crawled through and stood upon the grounds of a neighbouring estate. For the moment he was free. He put on his cap against the chilly November wind, and set out along the half-mile road to town.

Eastchester was a suburban farming community, with a small shoe factory. The institutions which pandered to the factory workers were the ones patronized by the boys – a movie house, a quick-lunch wagon on wheels known as the Dog and the Bostonian Candy Kitchen. Basil tried the Dog first and happened immediately upon a prospect.

This was Bugs Brown, a hysterical boy, subject to fits and strenuously avoided. Years later he became a brilliant lawyer, but at that time he was considered by the boys of St Regis to be a typical lunatic because of the peculiar series of sounds with which he assuaged his nervousness all day long.

He consorted with boys younger than himself, who were without the prejudices of their elders, and was in the company of several when Basil came in.

'Who-ee!' he cried. 'Ee-ee-ee!' He put his hand over his mouth and bounced it quickly, making a wah-wah-wah sound. 'It's Bossy Lee! It's Bossy Lee! It's Boss-Boss-Boss-Boss-Bossy Lee!'

'Wait a minute, Bugs,' said Basil anxiously, half afraid that Bugs would go finally crazy before he could persuade him to come to town. 'Say, Bugs, listen. Don't, Bugs – wait a minute. Can you come up to New York Saturday afternoon?'

'Whe-ee-ee!' cried Bugs to Basil's distress. 'Wee-ee-ee!'

'Honestly, Bugs, tell me, can you? We could go up together if you could go.'

'I've got to see a doctor,' said Bugs, suddenly calm. 'He wants to see how crazy I am.'

'Can't you have him see about it some other day?' said Basil without humour.

'Whee-ee-ee!' cried Bugs.

'All right then,' said Basil hastily. 'Have you seen Fat Gaspar in town?'

Bugs was lost in shrill noise, but someone had seen Fat: Basil was directed to the Bostonian Candy Kitchen.

This was a gaudy paradise of cheap sugar. Its odour, heavy and sickly and calculated to bring out a sticky sweat upon an adult's palms, hung suffocatingly over the whole vicinity and met one like a strong moral dissuasion at the door. Inside, beneath a pattern of flies, material as black point lace, a line of boys sat eating heavy dinners of banana splits, maple nut, and chocolate marshmallow nut sundaes. Basil found Fat Gaspar at a table on the side.

Fat Gaspar was at once Basil's most unlikely and most ambitious quest. He was considered a nice fellow – in fact he was so pleasant that he had been courteous to Basil and had spoken to him politely all fall. Basil realized that he was like that to everyone, yet it was just possible that Fat liked him, as people used to in the past, and he was driven desperately to take a chance. But it was undoubtedly a presumption, and as he approached the table and saw the stiffened faces which the other two boys turned towards him, Basil's hope diminished.

'Say, Fat –' he said, and hesitated. Then he burst forth suddenly. 'I'm on bounds, but I ran off because I had to see you. Doctor Bacon told me I could go to New York Saturday if I could get two other boys to go. I asked Bugs Brown and he couldn't go, and I thought I'd ask you.'

He broke off, furiously embarrassed, and waited. Suddenly the two boys with Fat burst into a shout of laughter.

'Bugs wasn't crazy enough!'

Fat Gaspar hesitated. He couldn't go to New York Saturday and ordinarily he would have refused without offending. He had nothing against Basil; nor, indeed, against anybody; but boys have only a certain resistance to public opinion and he was influenced by the contemptuous laughter of the others.

'I don't want to go,' he said indifferently. 'Why do you want to ask *me*?'

Then, half in shame, he gave a deprecatory little laugh and bent over his ice cream.

'I just thought I'd ask you,' said Basil.

Turning quickly away, he went to the counter and in a hollow and unfamiliar voice ordered a strawberry sundae. He ate it mechanically, hearing occasional whispers and snickers from the table behind. Still in a daze, he started to walk out without paying his check, but the clerk called him back and he was conscious of more derisive laughter.

For a moment he hesitated whether to go back to the table and hit one of those boys in the face, but he saw nothing to be gained. They would say the truth – that he had done it because he couldn't get anybody to go to New York. Clenching his fists with impotent rage, he walked from the store.

He came immediately upon his third prospect, Treadway. Treadway had entered St Regis late in the year and had been put in to room with Basil the week before. The fact that Treadway hadn't witnessed his humiliations of the autumn encouraged Basil to behave naturally towards him, and their relations had been, if not intimate, at least tranquil.

'Hey, Treadway,' he called, still excited from the affair in the Bostonian, 'can you come up to New York to a show Saturday afternoon?'

He stopped, realizing that Treadway was in the company of Brick Wales, a boy he had had a fight with and one of his bitterest enemies. Looking from one to the other, Basil saw a look of impatience in Treadway's face and a faraway expression in Brick Wales's, and he realized what must have been happening. Treadway, making his way into the life of the school, had just been enlightened as to the status of his room-mate. Like Fat Gaspar, rather than acknowledge himself eligible to such an intimate request, he preferred to cut their friendly relations short.

'Not on your life,' he said briefly. 'So long.' The two walked past him into the Candy Kitchen.

Had these slights, so much the bitterer for their lack of

passion, been visited upon Basil in September, they would have been unbearable. But since then he had developed a shell of hardness which, while it did not add to his attractiveness, spared him certain delicacies of torture. In misery enough, and despair and self-pity, he went the other way along the street for a little distance until he could control the violent contortions of his face. Then, taking a roundabout route, he started back to school.

He reached the adjoining estate, intending to go back the way he had come. Half-way through a hedge, he heard foot-steps approaching along the sidewalk and stood motionless, fearing the proximity of masters. Their voices grew nearer and louder; before he knew it he was listening with horrified fas-cination:

'– so, after he tried Bugs Brown, the poor nut asked Fat Gaspar to go with him and Fat said, "What do you ask me for?" It serves him right if he couldn't get anybody at all.'

It was the dismal but triumphant voice of Lewis Crum.

3

Up in his room, Basil found a package lying on his bed. He knew its contents and for a long time he had been eagerly ex-pecting it, but such was his depression that he opened it list-lessly. It was a series of eight colour reproductions of Harrison Fisher girls 'on glossy paper, without printing or advertising matter and suitable for framing'.

The pictures were named Dora, Marguerite, Babette, Lucille, Gretchen, Rose, Katherine, and Mina. Two of them – Marguerite and Rose – Basil looked at, slowly tore up, and dropped in the waste-basket, as one who disposes of the inferior pups from a litter. The other six he pinned at intervals around the room. Then he lay down on his bed and regarded them.

Dora, Lucille, and Katherine were blonde; Gretchen was medium; Babette and Mina were dark. After a few minutes, he found that he was looking oftenest at Dora and Babette and, to a lesser extent, at Gretchen, though the latter's Dutch cap seemed unromantic and precluded the element of mystery. Babette, a dark little violet-eyed beauty in a tight-fitting hat, attracted him most; his eyes came to rest on her at last.

'Babette,' he whispered to himself – 'beautiful Babette.'

The sound of the word, so melancholy and suggestive, like 'Vilia' or 'I'm happy at Maxim's' on the phonograph, softened him and, turning over on his face, he sobbed into the pillow. He took hold of the bed rails over his head and, sobbing and straining, began to talk to himself brokenly – how he hated them and whom he hated – he listed a dozen – and what he would do to them when he was great and powerful. In previous moments like these he had always rewarded Fat Gaspar for his kindness, but now he was like the rest. Basil set upon him, pummelling him unmercifully, or laughed sneeringly when he passed him blind and begging on the street.

He controlled himself as he heard Treadway come in, but did not move or speak. He listened as the other moved about the room, and after a while became conscious that there was an unusual opening of closets and bureau drawers. Basil turned over, his arm concealing his tear-stained face. Treadway had an armful of shirts in his hand.

'What are you doing?' Basil demanded.

His room-mate looked at him stonily. 'I'm moving in with Wales,' he said.

'Oh!'

Treadway went on with his packing. He carried out a suitcase full, then another, took down some pennants and dragged his trunk into the hall. Basil watched him bundle his toilet things into a towel and take one last survey about the room's new barrenness to see if there was anything forgotten.

'Good-bye,' he said to Basil, without a ripple of expression on his face.

'Good-bye.'

Treadway went out. Basil turned over once more and choked into the pillow.

'Oh, poor Babette!' he cried huskily. 'Poor little Babette! Poor little Babette!'

Babette, svelte and piquante, looked down at him coquettishly from the wall.

4

Doctor Bacon, sensing Basil's predicament and perhaps the extremity of his misery, arranged it that he should go into New York, after all. He went in the company of Mr Rooney, the football coach and history teacher. At twenty Mr Rooney had hesitated for some time between joining the police force and having his way paid through a small New England college; in fact he was a hard specimen and Doctor Bacon was planning to get rid of him at Christmas. Mr Rooney's contempt for Basil was founded on the latter's ambiguous and unreliable conduct on the football field during the past season – he had consented to take him to New York for reasons of his own.

Basil sat meekly beside him on the train, glancing past Mr Rooney's bulky body at the Sound and the fallow fields of Westchester County. Mr Rooney finished his newspaper, folded it up and sank into a moody silence. He had eaten a large breakfast and the exigencies of time had not allowed him to work it off with exercise. He remembered that Basil was a fresh boy, and it was time he did something fresh and could be called to account. This reproachless silence annoyed him.

'Lee,' he said suddenly, with a thinly assumed air of friendly interest, 'why don't you get wise to yourself?'

'What, sir?' Basil was startled from his excited trance of this morning.

'I said why don't you get wise to yourself?' said Mr Rooney in a somewhat violent tone. 'Do you want to be the butt of the school all your time here?'

'No, I don't,' Basil was chilled. Couldn't all this be left behind for just one day?

'You oughtn't to get so fresh all the time. A couple of times in history class I could just about have broken your neck.' Basil could think of no appropriate answer. 'Then out playing football,' continued Mr Rooney, '– you didn't have any nerve. You could play better than a lot of 'em when you wanted, like that day against the Pomfret seconds, but you lost your nerve.'

'I shouldn't have tried for the second team,' said Basil. 'I was too light. I should have stayed on the third.'

'You were yellow, that was all the trouble. You ought to get wise to yourself. In class, you're always thinking of something else. If you don't study, you'll never get to college.'

'I'm the youngest boy in the fifth form,' Basil said rashly.

'You think you're pretty bright, don't you?' He eyed Basil ferociously. Then something seemed to occur to him that changed his attitude and they rode for a while in silence. When the train began to run through the thickly clustered communities near New York, he spoke again in a milder voice and with an air of having considered the matter for a long time:

'Lee, I'm going to trust you.'

'Yes, sir.'

'You go and get some lunch and then go on to your show. I've got some business of my own I got to attend to, and when I've finished I'll try to get to the show. If I can't, I'll anyhow meet you outside.' Basil's heart leaped up. 'Yes, sir.'

'I don't want you to open your mouth about this at school — I mean, about me doing some business of my own.'

'No, sir.'

'We'll see if you can keep your mouth shut for once,' he said, making it fun. Then he added, on a note of moral sternness, 'And no drinks, you understand that?'

'Oh, no, sir!' The idea shocked Basil. He had never tasted a drink, nor even contemplated the possibility, save the intangible and non-alcoholic champagne of his café dreams.

On the advice of Mr Rooney he went for luncheon to the Manhattan Hotel, near the station, where he ordered a club sandwich, French fried potatoes, and a chocolate parfait. Out of the corner of his eye he watched the nonchalant, debonair, blasé New Yorkers at neighbouring tables, investing them with a romance by which these possible fellow citizens of his from the Middle West lost nothing. School had fallen from him like a burden; it was no more than an unheeded clamour, faint and far away. He even delayed opening the letter from the morning's mail which he found in his pocket, because it was addressed to him at school.

He wanted another chocolate parfait, but being reluctant to bother the busy waiter any more, he opened the letter and spread it before him instead. It was from his mother :

Dear Basil :

This is written in great haste, as I didn't want to frighten you by telegraphing. Grandfather is going abroad to take the waters and he wants you and me to come too. The idea is that you'll go to school at Grenoble or Montreux for the rest of the year and learn the language and we'll be close by. That is, if you want to. I know how you like St Regis and playing football and baseball, and of course there would be none of that; but on the other hand, it would be a nice change, even if it postponed your entering Yale by an extra year. So, as usual, I want you to do just as you like. We will be leaving home almost as soon as you get this and will come to the Waldorf in New York, where you can come in and see us for a few days, even if you decide to stay. Think it over, dear.

With love to my dearest boy,
Mother.

Basil got up from his chair with a dim idea of walking over to the Waldorf and having himself locked up safely until his mother came. Then, impelled to some gesture, he raised his voice and in one of his first basso notes called boomingly and without reticence for the waiter. No more St Regis ! No more St Regis ! He was almost strangling with happiness.

'Oh, gosh !' he cried to himself. 'Oh, golly ! Oh, gosh ! Oh, gosh !' No more Doctor Bacon and Mr Rooney and Brick Wales and Fat Gaspar. No more Bugs Brown and on bounds and being called Bossy. He need no longer hate them, for they were impotent shadows in the stationary world that he was sliding away from, sliding past, waving his hand. 'Good-bye !' he pitied them. 'Good-bye !'

It required the din of Forty-second Street to sober his maudlin joy. With his hand on his purse to guard against the omnipresent pickpocket, he moved cautiously towards Broadway. What a day! He would tell Mr Rooney – Why, he needn't ever go back! Or perhaps it would be better to go back and let them know what he was going to do, while they went on and on in the dismal, dreary round of school.

He found the theatre and entered the lobby with its powdery feminine atmosphere of a matinée. As he took out his ticket, his gaze was caught and held by a sculptured profile a few feet away. It was that of a well-built blond young man of about twenty with a strong chin and direct grey eyes. Basil's brain spun wildly for a moment and then came to rest upon a name – more than a name – upon a legend, a sign in the sky. What a day! He had never seen the young man before, but from a thousand pictures he knew beyond the possibility of a doubt that it was Ted Fay, the Yale football captain, who had almost single-handed beaten Harvard and Princeton last fall. Basil felt a sort of exquisite pain. The profile turned away; the crowd revolved; the hero disappeared. But Basil would know all through the next hours that Ted Fay was here too.

In the rustling, whispering, sweet-smelling darkness of the theatre he read the programme. It was the show of all shows that he wanted to see, and until the curtain actually rose the programme itself had a curious sacredness – a prototype of the thing itself. But when the curtain rose it became waste paper to be dropped carelessly to the floor.

Act 1. The Village Green of a Small Town near New York

It was too bright and blinding to comprehend all at once, and it went so fast that from the very first Basil felt he had missed things; he would make his mother take him again when she came – next week – tomorrow.

An hour passed. It was very sad at this point – a sort of gay sadness, but sad. The girl – the man. What kept them apart even now? Oh, those tragic errors and misconceptions. So sad. Couldn't they look into each other's eyes and *see*?

In a blaze of light and sound, of resolution, anticipation and imminent trouble, the act was over.

23

He went out. He looked for Ted Fay and thought he saw him leaning rather moodily on the plush wall at the rear of the theatre, but he could not be sure. He bought cigarettes and lit one, but fancying at the first puff he heard a blare of music he rushed back inside.

Act 2. *The Foyer of the Hotel Astor*

Yes, she was, indeed, like a song – a Beautiful Rose of the Night. The waltz buoyed her up, brought her with it to a point of aching beauty and then let her slide back to life across its last bars as a leaf slants to earth across the air. The high life of New York! Who could blame her if she was carried away by the glitter of it all, vanishing into the bright morning of the amber window borders or into distant and entrancing music as the door opened and closed that led to the ballroom? The toast of the shining town.

Half an hour passed. Her true love brought her roses like herself and she threw them scornfully at his feet. She laughed and turned to the other, and danced – danced madly, wildly. Wait! That delicate treble among the thin horns, the low curving note from the great strings. There it was again, poignant and aching, sweeping like a great gust of emotion across the stage, catching her again like a leaf helpless in the wind:

> 'Rose – Rose – Rose of the night,
> When the spring moon is bright you'll be fair –'

A few minutes later, feeling oddly shaken and exalted, Basil drifted outside with the crowd. The first thing upon which his eyes fell was the almost forgotten and now curiously metamorphosed spectre of Mr Rooney.

Mr Rooney had, in fact, gone a little to pieces. He was, to begin with, wearing a different and much smaller hat than when he left Basil at noon. Secondly, his face had lost its somewhat gross aspect and turned a pure and even delicate white, and he was wearing his necktie and even portions of his shirt on the outside of his unaccountably wringing-wet overcoat. How, in the short space of four hours, Mr Rooney had got himself in such shape is explicable only by the pressure of confinement in a boys' school upon a fiery outdoor spirit. Mr Rooney was born to toil under the clear light of heaven and, perhaps half-consciously, he was headed towards his inevitable destiny.

'Lee,' he said dimly, 'you ought to get wise to y'self. I'm going to put you wise y'self.'

To avoid the ominous possibility of being put wise to himself in the lobby, Basil uneasily changed the subject.

'Aren't you coming to the show?' he asked, flattering Mr Rooney by implying that he was in any condition to come to the show. 'It's a wonderful show.'

Mr Rooney took off his hat, displaying wringing-wet matted hair. A picture of reality momentarily struggled for development in the back of his brain.

'We got to get back to school,' he said in a sombre and unconvinced voice.

'But there's another act,' protested Basil in horror. 'I've got to stay for the last act.'

Swaying, Mr Rooney looked at Basil, dimly realizing that he had put himself in the hollow of this boy's hand.

'All righ',' he admitted. 'I'm going to get somethin' to eat. I'll wait for you next door.'

He turned abruptly, reeled a dozen steps, and curved dizzily into a bar adjoining the theatre. Considerably shaken, Basil went back inside.

Act 3. The Roof Garden of Mr Van Astor's House.
Night

Half an hour passed. Everything was going to be all right, after all. The comedian was at his best now, with the glad appropriateness of laughter after tears, and there was a promise of felicity in the bright tropical sky. One lovely plaintive duet, and then abruptly the long moment of incomparable beauty was over.

Basil went into the lobby and stood in thought while the

crowd passed out. His mother's letter and the show had cleared his mind of bitterness and vindictiveness – he was his old self and he wanted to do the right thing. He wondered if it was the right thing to get Mr Rooney back to school. He walked towards the saloon, slowed up as he came to it and, gingerly opening the swinging door, took a quick peer inside. He saw only that Mr Rooney was not one of those drinking at the bar. He walked down the street a little way, came back and tried again. It was as if he thought the doors were teeth to bite him, for he had the old-fashioned Middle-Western boy's horror of the saloon. The third time he was successful. Mr Rooney was sound asleep at a table in the back of the room.

Outside again Basil walked up and down, considering. He would give Mr Rooney half an hour. If, at the end of that time, he had not come out, he would go back to school. After all, Mr Rooney had laid for him ever since football season – Basil was simply washing his hands of the whole affair, as in a day or so he would wash his hands of school.

He had made several turns up and down, when glancing up an alley that ran beside the theatre his eye was caught by the sign, Stage Entrance. He could watch the actors come forth.

He waited. Women streamed by him, but those were the days before Glorification and he took these drab people for wardrobe women or something. Then suddenly a girl came out and with her a man, and Basil turned and ran a few steps up the street as if afraid they would recognize him – and ran back, breathing as if with a heart attack – for the girl, a radiant little beauty of nineteen, was Her and the young man by her side was Ted Fay.

Arm in arm, they walked past him, and irresistibly Basil followed. As they walked, she leaned towards Ted Fay in a way that gave them a fascinating air of intimacy. They crossed Broadway and turned into the Knickerbocker Hotel, and twenty feet behind them Basil followed, in time to see them go into a long room set for afternoon tea. They sat at a table for two, spoke vaguely to a waiter, and then, alone at last, bent eagerly towards each other. Basil saw that Ted Fay was holding her gloved hand.

The tea room was separated only by a hedge of potted firs from the main corridor. Basil went along this to a lounge which was almost up against their table and sat down.

Her voice was low and faltering, less certain than it had been in the play, and very sad: 'Of course I do, Ted.' For a long time, as their conversation continued, she repeated. 'Of course I do' or 'But I do, Ted.' Ted Fay's remarks were too low for Basil to hear.

'– says next month, and he won't be put off any more. . . . I do in a way, Ted. It's hard to explain, but he's done everything for mother and me. . . . There's no use kidding myself. It was a foolproof part and any girl he gave it to was made right then and there. . . . He's been awfully thoughtful. He's done everything for me.'

Basil's ears were sharpened by the intensity of his emotion; now he could hear Ted Fay's voice too:

'And you say you love me.'

'But don't you see I promised to marry him more than a year ago.'

'Tell him the truth – that you love me. Ask him to let you off.'

'This isn't musical comedy, Ted.'

'That was a mean one,' he said bitterly.

'I'm sorry, dear, Ted darling, but you're driving me crazy going on this way. You're making it so hard for me.'

'I'm going to leave New Haven, anyhow.'

'No, you're not. You're going to stay and play baseball this spring. Why, you're an ideal to all those boys! Why, if you –'

He laughed shortly. 'You're a fine one to talk about ideals.'

'Why not? I'm living up to my responsibility to Beltzman; you've got to make up your mind just like I have – that we can't have each other.'

'Jerry! Think what you're doing! All my life, whenever I hear that waltz –'

Basil got to his feet and hurried down the corridor, through the lobby and out of the hotel. He was in a state of wild emotional confusion. He did not understand all he had heard,

27

but from his clandestine glimpse into the privacy of these two, with all the world that his short experience could conceive of at their feet, he had gathered that life for everybody was a struggle, sometimes magnificent from a distance, but always difficult and surprisingly simple and a little sad.

They would go on. Ted Fay would go back to Yale, put her picture in his bureau drawer and knock out home runs with the bases full this spring – at 8.30 the curtain would go up and She would miss something warm and young out of her life, something she had had this afternoon.

It was dark outside and Broadway was a blazing forest fire as Basil walked slowly along towards the point of brightest light. He looked up at the great intersecting planes of radiance with a vague sense of approval and possession. He would see it a lot now, lay his restless heart upon this greater restlessness of a nation – he would come whenever he could get off from school.

But that was all changed – he was going to Europe. Suddenly Basil realized that he wasn't going to Europe. He could not forgo the moulding of his own destiny just to alleviate a few months of pain. The conquest of the successive worlds of school, college and New York – why, that was his true dream that he had carried from boyhood into adolescence, and because of the jeers of a few boys he had been about to abandon it and run ignominiously up a back alley! He shivered violently, like a dog coming out of the water, and simultaneously he was reminded of Mr Rooney.

A few minutes later he walked into the bar, past the quizzical eyes of the bartender and up to the table where Mr Rooney still sat asleep. Basil shook him gently, then firmly. Mr Rooney stirred and perceived Basil.

'G'wise to yourself,' he muttered drowsily. 'G'wise to yourself an' let me alone.'

'I am wise to myself,' said Basil. 'Honest, I am wise to myself, Mr Rooney. You got to come with me into the washroom and get cleaned up, and then you can sleep on the train again, Mr Rooney. Come on, Mr Rooney, please –'

5

It was a long hard time. Basil got on bounds again in December and wasn't free again until March. An indulgent mother had given him no habits of work and this was almost beyond the power of anything but life itself to remedy, but he made numberless new starts and failed and tried again.

He made friends with a new boy named Maplewood after Christmas, but they had a silly quarrel; and through the winter term, when a boys' school is shut in with itself and only partly assuaged from its natural savagery by indoor sports, Basil was snubbed and slighted a good deal for his real and imaginary sins, and he was much alone. But on the other hand, there was Ted Fay, and Rose of the Night on the phonograph – 'All my life whenever I hear that waltz' – and the remembered lights of New York, and the thought of what he was going to do in football next autumn and the glamorous image of Yale and the hope of spring in the air.

Fat Gaspar and a few others were nice to him now. Once when he and Fat walked home together by accident from downtown they had a long talk about actresses – a talk that Basil was wise enough not to presume upon afterwards. The smaller boys suddenly decided that they approved of him, and a master who had hitherto disliked him put his hand on his shoulder walking to a class one day. They would all forget eventually – maybe during the summer. There would be new fresh boys in September; he would have a clean start next year.

One afternoon in February, playing basketball, a great thing happened. He and Brick Wales were at forward on the second team and in the fury of the scrimmage the gymnasium echoed with sharp slapping contacts and shrill cries.

'Here yar!'

'Bill! Bill!'

Basil had dribbled the ball down the court and Brick Wales, free, was crying for it.

'Here yar! Lee! Hey! Lee-y!'

Basil: The Freshest Boy

Lee-y!

Basil flushed and made a poor pass. He had been called by a nickname. It was a poor makeshift, but it was something more than the stark bareness of his surname or a term of derision. Brick Wales went on playing, unconscious that he had done anything in particular or that he had contributed to the events by which another boy was saved from the army of the bitter, the selfish, the neurasthenic and the unhappy. It isn't given to us to know those rare moments when people are wide open and the lightest touch can wither or heal. A moment too late and we can never reach them any more in this world. They will not be cured by our most efficacious drugs or slain with our sharpest swords.

Lee-y! It could scarcely be pronounced. But Basil took it to bed with him that night, and thinking of it, holding it to him happily to the last, fell easily to sleep.

Josephine: A Woman with a Past

[1930]

I

Driving slowly through New Haven, two of the young girls became alert. Josephine and Lillian darted soft frank glances into strolling groups of three or four undergraduates, into larger groups on corners, which swung about as one man to stare at their receding heads. Believing that they recognized an acquaintance in a solitary loiterer, they waved wildly, whereupon the youth's mouth fell open, and as they turned the next corner he made a dazed dilatory gesture with his hand. They laughed. 'We'll send him a post card when we get back to school tonight, to see if it really was him.'

Adele Craw, sitting on one of the little seats, kept on talking to Miss Chambers, the chaperon. Glancing sideways at her, Lillian winked at Josephine without batting an eye, but Josephine had gone into a reverie.

This was New Haven – city of her adolescent dreams, of glittering proms where she would move on air among men as intangible as the tunes they danced to. City sacred as Mecca, shining as Paris, hidden as Timbuktu. Twice a year the life-blood of Chicago, her home, flowed into it, and twice a year flowed back, bringing Christmas or bringing summer. Bingo, bingo, bingo, that's the lingo; love of mine, I pine for one of your glances; the darling boy on the left there; underneath the stars I wait.

Seeing it for the first time, she found herself surprisingly unmoved – the men they passed seemed young and rather bored with the possibilities of the day, glad of anything to stare at; seemed undynamic and purposeless against the background of bare elms, lakes of dirty snow and buildings crowded together under the February sky. A wisp of hope, a well-turned-out derby-crowned man, hurrying with stick and suitcase towards the station, caught her attention, but his reciprocal glance was too startled, too ingenuous. Josephine wondered at the extent of her own disillusionment.

She was exactly seventeen and she was blasé. Already she had been a sensation and a scandal; she had driven mature men to a state of disequilibrium; she had, it was said, killed her grandfather, but as he was over eighty at the time perhaps he just died. Here and there in the Middle West were discouraged little spots which upon inspection turned out to be the youths who had once looked full into her green and wistful eyes. But her love affair of last summer had ruined her faith in the all-sufficiency of men. She had grown bored with the waning September days – and it seemed as though it had happened once too often. Christmas with its provocative shortness, its travelling glee clubs, had brought no one new. There remained to her only a persistent, a physical hope; hope in her stomach that there was someone whom she would love more than he loved her.

They stopped at a sporting-goods store and Adele Craw, a pretty girl with clear honourable eyes and piano legs, purchased the sporting equipment which was the reason for their trip – they were the spring hockey committee for the school. Adele was in addition the president of the senior class and the school's ideal girl. She had lately seen a change for the better in Josephine Perry – rather as an honest citizen might guilelessly approve a speculator retired on his profits. On the other hand, Adele was simply incomprehensible to Josephine – admirable, without doubt, but a member of another species. Yet with the charming adaptability that she had hitherto reserved for men, Josephine was trying hard not to disillusion her, trying to be honestly interested in the small, neat, organized politics of the school.

Two men who had stood with their backs to them at another counter turned to leave the store, when they caught sight of Miss Chambers and Adele. Immediately they came forward. The one who spoke to Miss Chambers was thin and rigid of face. Josephine recognized him as Miss Brereton's nephew, a student at New Haven, who had spent several week-ends with his aunt at the school. The other man Josephine had never seen before. He was tall and broad, with blond curly hair and an open expression in which strength of purpose and a nice consideration were pleasantly mingled. It was not the sort of face that generally appealed to Josephine. The eyes were obviously without a secret, with a sidewise gambol, without a desperate flicker to show that they had a life of their own apart from the mouth's speech. The mouth itself was large and masculine; its smile was an act of kindness and control. It was rather with curiosity as to the sort of man who would be attentive to Adele Craw that Josephine continued to look at him, for his voice that obviously couldn't lie greeted Adele as if this meeting was the pleasant surprise of his day.

In a moment Josephine and Lillian were called over and introduced.

'This is Mr Waterbury' – that was Miss Brereton's nephew – 'and Mr Dudley Knowleton.'

Glancing at Adele, Josephine saw on her face an expression of tranquil pride, even of possession. Mr Knowleton spoke politely, but it was obvious that though he looked at the younger girls he did not quite see them. But since they were friends of Adele's he made suitable remarks, eliciting the fact that they were both coming down to New Haven to their first prom the following week. Who were their hosts? Sophomores; he knew them slightly. Josephine thought that was unnecessarily superior. Why, they were the charter members of the Loving Brothers' Association – Ridgeway Saunders and George Davey – and on the glee-club trip the girls they picked out to rush in each city considered themselves a sort of élite, second only to the girls they asked to New Haven.

'And oh, I've got some bad news for you,' Knowleton said to Adele. 'You may be leading the prom. Jack Coe went to the infirmary with appendicitis, and against my better judgement I'm the provisional chairman.' He looked apologetic. 'Being one of those stoneage dancers, the two-step king, I don't see how I ever got on the committee at all.'

When the car was on its way back to Miss Brereton's school, Josephine and Lillian bombarded Adele with questions.

'He's an old friend from Cincinnati,' she explained demurely. 'He's captain of the baseball team and he was last man for Skull and Bones.'

'You're going to the prom with him?'

'Yes. You see, I've known him all my life.'

Was there a faint implication in this remark that only those who had known Adele all her life knew her at her true worth?

'Are you engaged?' Lillian demanded.

Adele laughed. 'Mercy, I don't think of such matters! It doesn't seem to be time for that sort of thing yet, does it?' ('Yes,' interpolated Josephine silently.) 'We're just good friends. I think there can be a perfectly healthy friendship between a man and a girl without a lot of –'

'Mush,' supplied Lillian helpfully.

'Well, yes, but I don't like that word. I was going to say without a lot of sentimental romantic things that ought to come later.'

'Bravo, Adele!' said Miss Chambers somewhat perfunctorily.

But Josephine's curiosity was unappeased.

'Doesn't he say he's in love with you, and all that sort of thing?'

'Mercy, no! Dud doesn't believe in such stuff any more than I do. He's got enough to do at New Haven, serving on the committees and the team.'

'Oh!' said Josephine.

She was oddly interested. That two people who were attracted to each other should never even say anything about it but be content to 'not believe in such stuff', was something new in her experience. She had known girls who had no beaux, others who seemed to have no emotions, and still others who lied about what they thought and did; but here was a girl who spoke of the attentions of the last man tapped for Skull and Bones as if they were two of the limestone gargoyles that Miss Chambers had pointed out on the just completed Harkness Hall. Yet Adele seemed happy – happier than Josephine, who had always believed that boys and girls were made for nothing but each other, and as soon as possible.

In the light of his popularity and achievements, Knowleton seemed more attractive. Josephine wondered if he would remember her and dance with her at the prom, or if that depended on how well he knew her escort, Ridgeway Saunders. She tried to remember whether she had smiled at him when he was looking at her. If she had really smiled he would remember her and dance with her. She was still trying to be sure of that over her two French irregular verbs and her ten stanzas of the Ancient Mariner that night; but she was still uncertain when she fell asleep.

2

Three gay young sophomores, the founders of the Loving Brothers' Association, took a house together for Josephine, Lillian and a girl from Farmington and their three mothers. For the girls it was a first prom, and they arrived at New Haven with all the nervousness of the condemned; but a Sheffield fraternity tea in the afternoon yielded up such a plethora of boys from home, and boys who had visited there and friends of those boys, and new boys with unknown possibilities but obvious eagerness, that they were glowing with self-confidence as they poured into the glittering crowd that thronged the armoury at ten.

It was impressive; for the first time Josephine was at a function run by men upon men's standards – an outward projection of the New Haven world from which women were excluded and which went on mysteriously behind the scenes. She perceived that their three escorts, who had once seemed the very embodiments of worldliness, were modest fry in this relentless microcosm of accomplishment and success. A man's world! Looking around her at the glee-club concert, Josephine had felt a grudging admiration for the good fellowship, the good feeling. She envied Adele Craw, barely glimpsed in the dressing-room, for the position she automatically occupied by being

Dudley Knowleton's girl tonight. She envied her more stepping off under the draped bunting through a gateway of hydrangeas at the head of the grand march, very demure and faintly unpowdered in a plain white dress. She was temporarily the centre of all attention, and at the sight something that had long lain dormant in Josephine awakened – her sense of a problem, a scarcely defined possibility.

'Josephine,' Ridgeway Saunders began, 'you can't realize how happy I am now that it's come true. I've looked forward to this so long, and dreamed about it –'

She smiled up at him automatically, but her mind was elsewhere, and as the dance progressed the idea continued to obsess her. She was rushed from the beginning; to the men from the tea were added a dozen new faces, a dozen confident or timid voices, until, like all the more popular girls, she had her own queue trailing her about the room. Yet all this had happened to her before, and there was something missing. One might have ten men to Adele's two, but Josephine was abruptly aware that here a girl took on the importance of the man who had brought her.

She was discomforted by the unfairness of it. A girl earned her popularity by being beautiful and charming. The more beautiful and charming she was, the more she could afford to disregard public opinion. It seemed absurd that simply because Adele had managed to attach a baseball captain, who mightn't know anything about girls at all, or be able to judge their attractions, she should be thus elevated in spite of her thick ankles, her rather too pinkish face.

Josephine was dancing with Ed Bement from Chicago. He was her earliest beau, a flame of pigtail days in dancing school when one wore white cotton stockings, lace drawers with a waist attached and ruffled dresses with the inevitable sash.

'What's the matter with me?' she asked Ed, thinking aloud. 'For months I've felt as if I were a hundred years old, and I'm just seventeen and that party was only seven years ago.'

'You've been in love a lot since then,' Ed said.

'I haven't,' she protested indignantly. 'I've had a lot of silly stories started about me, without any foundation, usually by girls who were jealous.'

'Jealous of what?'

'Don't get fresh,' she said tartly. 'Dance me near Lillian.'

Dudley Knowleton had just cut in on Lillian. Josephine spoke to her friend; then waiting until their turns would bring them face to face over a space of seconds, she smiled at Knowleton. This time she made sure that smile intersected as well as met glance, that he passed beside the circumference of her fragrant charm. If this had been named like French perfume of a later day it might have been called 'Please'. He bowed and smiled back; a minute later he cut in on her.

It was in an eddy in a corner of the room and she danced slower so that he adapted himself, and for a moment they went around in a slow circle.

'You looked so sweet leading the march with Adele,' she told him. 'You seemed so serious and kind, as if the others were a lot of children. Adele looked sweet, too.' And she added on an inspiration, 'At school I've taken her for a model.'

'You have!' She saw him conceal his sharp surprise as he said, 'I'll have to tell her that.'

He was handsomer than she had thought, and behind his cordial good manners there was a sort of authority. Though he was correctly attentive to her, she saw his eyes search the room quickly to see if all went well; he spoke quietly, in passing, to the orchestra leader, who came down deferentially to the edge of his dais. Last man for Bones. Josephine knew what that meant – her father had been Bones. Ridgeway Saunders and the rest of the Loving Brothers' Association would certainly not be Bones. She wondered, if there had been a Bones for girls, whether she would be tapped – or Adele Craw with her ankles, symbol of solidity.

> Come on o-ver here,
> Want to have you near;
> Get a wel-come heart-y.
> Come on join the part-y,

'I wonder how many boys here have taken you for a model,'

she said. 'If I were a boy you'd be exactly what I'd like to be. Except I'd be terribly bothered having girls falling in love with me all the time.'

'They don't,' he said simply. 'They never have.'

'Oh yes – but they hide it because they're so impressed with you, and they're afraid of Adele.'

'Adele wouldn't object.' And he added hastily, '– if it ever happened. Adele doesn't believe in being serious about such things.'

'Are you engaged to her?'

He stiffened a little. 'I don't believe in being engaged till the right time comes.'

'Neither do I,' agreed Josephine readily. 'I'd rather have one good friend than a hundred people hanging around being mushy all the time.'

'Is that what that crowd does that keeps following you around tonight?'

'What crowd?' she asked innocently.

'The fifty per cent of the sophomore class that's rushing you.'

'A lot of parlour snakes,' she said ungratefully.

Josephine was radiantly happy now as she turned beautifully through the newly enchanted hall in the arms of the chairman of the prom committee. Even this extra time with him she owed to the awe which he inspired in her entourage; but a man cut in eventually and there was a sharp fall in her elation. The man was impressed that Dudley Knowleton had danced with her; he was more respectful, and his modulated admiration bored her. In a little while, she hoped, Dudley Knowleton would cut back, but as midnight passed, dragging on another hour with it, she wondered if after all it had only been a courtesy to a girl from Adele's school. Since then Adele had probably painted him a neat little landscape of Josephine's past. When finally he approached her she grew tense and watchful, a state which made her exteriorly pliant and tender and quiet. But instead of dancing he drew her into the edge of a row of boxes.

'Adele had an accident on the cloakroom steps. She turned her ankle a little and tore her stocking on a nail. She'd like to borrow a pair from you because you're staying near here and we're way out at the Lawn Club.'

'Of course.'

'I'll run over with you – I have a car outside.'

'But you're busy, you mustn't bother.'

'Of course I'll go with you.'

There was thaw in the air; a hint of thin and lucid spring hovered delicately around the elms and cornices of buildings whose bareness and coldness had so depressed her the week before. The night had a quality of asceticism, as if the essence of masculine struggle were seeping everywhere through the little city where men of three centuries had brought their energies and aspirations for winnowing. And Dudley Knowleton sitting beside her, dynamic and capable, was symbolic of it all. It seemed that she had never met a man before.

'Come in, please,' she said as he went up the steps of the house with her. 'They've made it very comfortable.'

There was an open fire burning in the dark parlour. When she came downstairs with the stockings she went in and stood beside him, very still for a moment, watching it with him. Then she looked up, still silent, looked down, looked at him again.

'Did you get the stockings?' he asked, moving a little.

'Yes,' she said breathlessly. 'Kiss me for being so quick.'

He laughed as if she said something witty and moved towards the door. She was smiling and her disappointment was deeply hidden as they got into the car.

'It's been wonderful meeting you,' she told him. 'I can't tell you how many ideas I've gotten from what you said.'

'But I haven't any ideas.'

'You have. All that about not getting engaged till the proper time comes. I haven't had much opportunity to talk to a man like you. Otherwise my ideas would be different, I guess. I've just realized that I've been wrong about a lot of things. I used to want to be exciting. Now I want to help people.'

'Yes,' he agreed, 'that's very nice.'

He seemed about to say more when they arrived at the armoury. In their absence supper had begun; and crossing the great floor by his side, conscious of many eyes regarding them, Josephine wondered if people thought that they had been up to something.

'We're late,' said Knowleton when Adele went off to put on the stockings. 'The man you're with has probably given you up long ago. You'd better let me get you something here.'

'That would be too divine.'

Afterwards, back on the floor again, she moved in a sweet aura of abstraction. The followers of several departed belles merged with hers until now no girl on the floor was cut in on with such frequency. Even Miss Brereton's nephew, Ernest Waterbury, danced with her in stiff approval. Danced? With a tentative change of pace she simply swung from man to man in a sort of hands-right-and-left around the floor. She felt a sudden need to relax, and as if in answer to her mood a new man was presented, a tall, sleek Southerner with a persuasive note:

'You lovely creacha. I been strainin my eyes watchin your cameo face floatin round. You stand out above all these othuz like an Amehken Beauty Rose over a lot of field daisies.'

Dancing with him a second time, Josephine hearkened to his pleadings.

'All right. Let's go outside.'

'It wasn't outdaws I was considering,' he explained as they left the floor. 'I happen to have a mortgage on a nook right hee in the building.'

'All right.'

Book Chaffee, of Alabama, led the way through the cloak-room, through a passage to an inconspicuous door.

'This is the private apartment of my friend Sergeant Boone, instructa of the battery. He wanted to be particularly sure it'd be used as a nook tonight and not a readin room or anything like that.'

Opening the door he turned on a dim light; she came in and shut it behind her, and they faced each other.

'Mighty sweet,' he murmured. His tall face came down, his long arms wrapped around her tenderly, and very slowly so that their eyes met for quite a long time, he drew her up to

him. Josephine kept thinking that she had never kissed a Southern boy before.

They started apart at the sudden sound of a key turning in the lock outside. Then there was a muffed snicker followed by retreating footsteps, and Book sprang for the door and wrenched at the handle just as Josephine noticed that this was not only Sergeant Boone's parlour; it was his bedroom as well.

'Who was it?' she demanded. 'Why did they lock us in?'

'Some funny boy. I'd like to get my hands on him.'

'Will he come back?'

Book sat down on the bed to think. 'I couldn't say. Don't even know who it was. But if somebody on the committee came along it wouldn't look too good, would it?'

Seeing her expression change, he came over and put his arm around her. 'Don't you worry, honey. We'll fix it.'

She returned his kiss, briefly but without distraction. Then she broke away and went into the next apartment, which was hung with boots, uniform coats and various military equipment.

'There's a window up here,' she said. It was high in the wall and had not been opened for a long time. Book mounted on a chair and forced it ajar.

'About ten feet down,' he reported, after a moment, 'but there's a big pile of snow just underneath. You might get a nasty fall and you'll sure soak your shoes and stockin's.'

'We've got to get out,' Josephine said sharply.

'We'd better wait and give this funny man a chance –'

'I won't wait. I want to get out. Look – throw out all the blankets from the bed and I'll jump on that: or you jump first and spread them over the pile of snow.'

After that it was merely exciting. Carefully Book Chaffee wiped the dust from the window to protect her dress; then they were struck silent by a footstep that approached – and passed the outer door. Book jumped, and she heard him kicking profanely as he waded out of the soft drift below. He spread the blankets. At the moment when Josephine swung her legs out the window, there was the sound of voices outside the door and the key turned again in the lock. She landed softly, reaching for his hand, and convulsed with laughter they ran and skidded down the half block towards the corner, and reaching the entrance to the armoury, they stood panting for a moment, breathing in the fresh night. Book was reluctant to go inside.

'Why don't you let me conduct you where you're stayin? We can sit around and sort of recuperate.'

She hesitated, drawn towards him by the community of their late predicament; but something was calling her inside, as if the fulfilment of her elation awaited her there.

'No,' she decided.

As they went in she collided with a man in a great hurry, and looked up to recognize Dudley Knowleton.

'So sorry,' he said. 'Oh hello –'

'Won't you dance me over to my box?' she begged him impulsively. 'I've torn my dress.'

As they started off he said abstractedly: 'The fact is, a little mischief has come up and the buck has been passed to me. I was going along to see about it.'

Her heart raced wildly and she felt the need of being another sort of person immediately.

'I can't tell you how much it's meant meeting you. It would be wonderful to have one friend I could be serious with without being all mushy and sentimental. Would you mind if I wrote you a letter – I mean, would Adele mind?'

'Lord, no!' His smile had become utterly unfathomable to her. As they reached the box she thought of one more thing:

'Is it true that the baseball team is training at Hot Springs during Easter?'

'Yes. You going there?'

'Yes. Good night, Mr Knowleton.'

But she was destined to see him once more. It was outside the men's coat room, where she waited among a crowd of other pale survivors and their paler mothers, whose wrinkles had doubled and tripled with the passing night. He was explaining something to Adele, and Josephine heard the phrase, 'The door was locked, and the window open –'

Suddenly it occurred to Josephine that, meeting her coming

in damp and breathless, he must have guessed at the truth – and Adele would doubtless confirm his suspicion. Once again the spectre of her old enemy, the plain and jealous girl, arose before her. Shutting her mouth tight together she turned away.

But they had seen her, and Adele called to her in her cheerful ringing voice:

'Come say good night. You were so sweet about the stockings. Here's a girl you won't find doing shoddy, silly things, Dudley.' Impulsively she leaned and kissed Josephine on the cheek. 'You'll see I'm right, Dudley – next year she'll be the most respected girl in school.'

3

As things go in the interminable days of early March, what happened next happened quickly. The annual senior dance at Miss Brereton's school came on a night soaked through with spring, and all the junior girls lay awake listening to the sighing tunes from the gymnasium. Between the numbers, when boys up from New Haven and Princeton wandered about the grounds, cloistered glances looked down from dark open windows upon the vague figures.

Not Josephine, though she lay awake like the others. Such vicarious diversions had no place in the sober patterns she was spinning now from day to day; yet she might as well have been in the forefront of those who called down to the men and threw notes and entered into conversations, for destiny had suddenly turned against her and was spinning a dark web of its own.

> Lit-tle lady, don't be depressed and blue,
> After all, we're both in the same can-noo –

Dudley Knowleton was over in the gymnasium fifty yards away, but proximity to a man did not thrill her as it would have done a year ago – not, at least, in the same way. Life, she saw now, was a serious matter, and in the modest darkness a line of a novel ceaselessly recurred to her: 'He is a man fit to be the father of my children'. What were the seductive graces, the fast lines of a hundred parlour snakes compared to such realities. One couldn't go on forever kissing comparative strangers behind half-closed doors.

Under her pillow now were two letters, answers to her letters. They spoke in a bold round hand of the beginning of baseball practice; they were glad Josephine felt as she did about things; and the writer certainly looked forward to seeing her at Easter. Of all the letters she had ever received they were the most difficult from which to squeeze a single drop of heart's blood – one couldn't even read the 'Yours' of the subscription as 'Your' – but Josephine knew them by heart. They were precious because he had taken the time to write them; they were eloquent in the very postage stamp because he used so few.

She was restless in her bed – the music had begun again in the gymnasium:

> Oh, my love, I've waited so long for you,
> Oh, my love, I'm singing this song for you –
> Oh-h-h –

From the next room there was light laughter, and then from below a male voice, and a long interchange of comic whispers. Josephine recognized Lillian's laugh and the voices of two other girls. She could imagine them as they lay across the window in their nightgowns, their heads just showing from the open window. 'Come right down,' one boy kept saying. 'Don't be formal – come just as you are.'

There was a sudden silence, then a quick crunching of footsteps on gravel, a suppressed snicker and a scurry, and the sharp, protesting groan of several beds in the next room and the banging of a door down the hall. Trouble for somebody, maybe. A few minutes later Josephine's door half opened, she caught a glimpse of Miss Kwain against the dim corridor light, and then the door closed.

The next afternoon Josephine and four other girls, all of whom denied having breathed so much as a word into the night, were placed on probation. There was absolutely nothing to do about it. Miss Kwain had recognized their faces in the window and they were all from two rooms. It was an injustice, but it was nothing compared to what happened next. One week before Easter vacation the school motored off on a one-day trip to inspect a milk farm – all save the ones on probation. Miss Chambers, who sympathized with Josephine's misfortune, enlisted her services in entertaining Mr Ernest Waterbury, who was spending a week-end with his aunt. This was only vaguely better than nothing, for Mr Waterbury was a very dull, very priggish young man. He was so dull and so priggish that the following morning Josephine was expelled from school.

It happened like this: they had strolled in the grounds, they had sat down at a garden table and had tea. Ernest Waterbury had expressed a desire to see something in the chapel, just a few minutes before his aunt's car rolled up the drive. The chapel was reached by descending winding mock-medieval stairs; and, her shoes still wet from the garden, Josephine had slipped on the top step and fallen five feet directly into Mr Waterbury's unwilling arms, where she lay helpless, convulsed with irresistible laughter. It was in this position that Miss Brereton and the visiting trustee had found them.

'But I had nothing to do with it!' declared the ungallant Mr Waterbury. Flustered and outraged, he was packed back to New Haven, and Miss Brereton, connecting this with last week's sin, proceeded to lose her head. Josephine, humiliated and furious, lost hers, and Mr Perry, who happened to be in New York, arrived at the school the same night. At his passionate indignation, Miss Brereton collapsed and retracted, but the damage was done, and Josephine packed her trunk. Unexpectedly, monstrously, just as it had begun to mean something, her school life was over.

For the moment all her feelings were directed against Miss Brereton, and the only tears she shed at leaving were of anger and resentment. Riding with her father up to New York, she saw that while at first he had instinctively and whole-heartedly taken her part, he felt also a certain annoyance with her misfortune.

'We'll all survive,' he said. 'Unfortunately, even that old idiot

Miss Brereton will survive. She ought to be running a reform school.' He brooded for a moment. 'Anyhow, your mother arrives tomorrow and you and she go down to Hot Springs as you planned.'

'Hot Springs! 'Josephine cried, in a choked voice. 'Oh, no!'

'Why not?' he demanded in surprise. 'It seems the best thing to do. Give it a chance to blow over before you go back to Chicago.'

'I'd rather go to Chicago,' said Josephine breathlessly. 'Daddy, I'd much rather go to Chicago.'

'That's absurd. Your mother's started East and the arrangements are all made. At Hot Springs you can get out and ride and play golf and forget that old she-devil —'

'Isn't there another place in the East we could go? There's people I know going to Hot Springs who'll know all about this, people that I don't want to meet — girls from school.'

'Now, Jo, you keep your chin up — this is one of those times. Sorry I said that about letting it blow over in Chicago; if we hadn't made other plans we'd go back and face every old shrew and gossip in town right away. When anybody slinks off in a corner they think you've been up to something bad. If anybody says anything to you, you tell them the truth — what I said to Miss Brereton. You tell them she said you could come back and I damn well wouldn't let you go back.'

'They won't believe it.'

There would be, at all events, four days of respite at Hot Springs before the vacations of the schools. Josephine passed this time taking golf lessons from a professional so newly arrived from Scotland that he surely knew nothing of her misadventure; she even went riding with a young man one afternoon, feeling almost at home with him after his admission that he had flunked out of Princeton in February — a confidence, however, which she did not reciprocate in kind. But in the evenings, despite the young man's importunity, she stayed with her mother, feeling nearer to her than she ever had before.

But one afternoon in the lobby Josephine saw by the desk two dozen good-looking young men waiting by a stack of bat cases and bags, and knew that what she dreaded was at hand. She ran upstairs and with an invented headache dined there that night, but after dinner she walked restlessly around their apartment. She was ashamed not only of her situation but of her reaction to it. She had never felt any pity for the unpopular girls who skulked in dressing-rooms because they could attract no partners on the floor, or for girls who were outsiders at Lake Forest, and now she was like them – hiding miserably out of life. Alarmed lest already the change was written in her face, she paused in front of the mirror, fascinated as ever by what she found there.

'The darn fools!' she said aloud. And as she said it her chin went up and the faint cloud about her eyes lifted. The phrases of the myriad love letters she had received passed before her eyes; behind her, after all, was the reassurance of a hundred lost and pleading faces, of innumerable tender and pleading voices. Her pride flooded back into her till she could see the warm blood rushing up into her cheeks.

There was a knock at the door – it was the Princeton boy.

'How about slipping downstairs?' he proposed. 'There's a dance. It's full of E-lies, the whole Yale baseball team. I'll pick up one of them and introduce you and you'll have a big time. How about it?'

'All right, but I don't want to meet anybody. You'll just have to dance with me all evening.'

'You know that suits me.'

She hurried into a new spring evening dress of the frailest fairy blue. In the excitement of seeing herself in it, it seemed as if she had shed the old skin of winter and emerged a shining chrysalis with no stain; and going downstairs her feet fell softly just off the beat of the music from below. It was a tune from a play she had seen a week ago in New York, a tune with a future – ready for gaieties as yet unthought of, lovers not yet met. Dancing off, she was certain that life had innumerable beginnings. She had hardly gone ten steps when she was cut in upon by Dudley Knowleton.

'Why, Josephine!' He had never used her first name before –

he stood holding her hand. 'Why, I'm so glad to see you! I've been hoping and hoping you'd be here.'

She soared skyward on a rocket of surprise and delight. He was actually glad to see her – the expression on his face was obviously sincere. Could it be possible that he hadn't heard?

'Adele wrote me you might be here. She wasn't sure.'

– Then he knew and didn't care; he liked her anyhow.

'I'm in sackcloth and ashes,' she said.

'Well, they're very becoming to you.'

'You know what happened –' she ventured.

'I do. I wasn't going to say anything, but it's generally agreed that Waterbury behaved like a fool – and it's not going to be much help to him in the elections next month. Look – I want you to dance with some men who are just starving for a touch of beauty.'

Presently she was dancing with, it seemed to her, the entire team at once. Intermittently Dudley Knowleton cut back in, as well as the Princeton man, who was somewhat indignant at this unexpected competition. There were many girls from many schools in the room, but with an admirable team spirit the Yale men displayed a sharp prejudice in Josephine's favour; already she was pointed out from the chairs along the wall.

But interiorly she was waiting for what was coming, for the moment when she would walk with Dudley Knowleton into the warm, Southern night. It came naturally, just at the end of a number, and they strolled along an avenue of early-blooming lilacs and turned a corner and another corner . . .

'You were glad to see me, weren't you?' Josephine said.

'Of course.'

'I was afraid at first. I was sorriest about what happened at school because of you. I'd been trying so hard to be different – because of you.'

'You mustn't think of that school business any more. Everybody that matters knows you got a bad deal. Forget it and start over.'

'Yes,' she agreed tranquilly. She was happy. The breeze and

the scent of lilacs – that was she, lovely and intangible; the rustic bench where they sat and the trees – that was he, rugged and strong beside her, protecting her.

'I'd thought so much of meeting you here,' she said after a minute. 'You'd been so good for me, that I thought maybe in a different way I could be good for you – I mean I know ways of having a good time that you don't know. For instance, we've certainly got to go horseback riding by moonlight some night. That'll be fun.'

He didn't answer.

'I can really be very nice when I like somebody – that's really not often,' she interpolated hastily, 'not seriously. But I mean when I do feel seriously that a boy and I are really friends I don't believe in having a whole mob of other boys hanging around taking up time. I like to be with him all the time, all day and all evening, don't you?'

He stirred a little on the bench; he leaned forward with his elbows on his knees, looking at his strong hands. Her gently modulated voice sank a note lower.

'When I like anyone I don't even like dancing. It's sweeter to be alone.'

Silence for a moment.

'Well, you know' – he hesitated, frowning – 'as a matter of fact, I'm mixed up in a lot of engagements made some time ago with some people.' He floundered about unhappily. 'In fact, I won't even be at the hotel after tomorrow. I'll be at the house of some people down the valley – a sort of house party. As a matter of fact, Adele's getting here tomorrow.'

Absorbed in her own thoughts, she hardly heard him at first, but at the name she caught her breath sharply.

'We're both to be at this house party while we're here, and I imagine it's more or less arranged what we're going to do. Of course, in the daytime I'll be here for baseball practice.'

'I see.' Her lips were quivering. 'You won't be – you'll be with Adele.'

'I think that – more or less – I will. She'll – want to see you, of course.'

Another silence while he twisted his big fingers and she helplessly imitated the gesture.

'You were just sorry for me,' she said. 'You like Adele – much better.'

'Adele and I understand each other. She's been more or less my ideal since we were children together.'

'And I'm not your kind of girl?' Josephine's voice trembled with a sort of fright. 'I suppose because I've kissed a lot of boys and got a reputation for speed and raised the deuce.'

'It isn't that.'

'Yes, it is,' she declared passionately. 'I'm just paying for things.' She stood up. 'You'd better take me back inside so I can dance with the kind of boys that like me.'

She walked quickly down the path, tears of misery streaming from her eyes. He overtook her by the steps, but she only shook her head and said, 'Excuse me for being so fresh. I'll grow up – I got what was coming to me – it's all right.'

A little later when she looked around the floor for him he had gone – and Josephine realized with a shock that for the first time in her life, she had tried for a man and failed. But, save in the very young, only love begets love, and from the moment Josephine had perceived that his interest in her was merely kindness she realized the wound was not in her heart but in her pride. She would forget him quickly, but she would never forget what she had learned from him. There were two kinds of men, those you played with and those you might marry. And as this passed through her mind, her restless eyes wandered casually over the group of stags, resting very lightly on Mr Gordon Tinsley, the current catch of Chicago, reputedly the richest young man in the Middle West. He had never paid any attention to young Josephine until tonight. Ten minutes ago he had asked her to go driving with him tomorrow.

But he did not attract her – and she decided to refuse. One mustn't run through people, and, for the sake of a romantic half-hour, trade a possibility that might develop – quite seriously – later, at the proper time. She did not know that this was the first mature thought that she had ever had in her life, but it was.

The orchestra were packing their instruments and the Princeton man was still at her ear, still imploring her to walk out with him into the night. Josephine knew without cogitation which sort of man he was – and the moon was bright even on the windows. So with a certain sense of relaxation she took his arm and they strolled out to the pleasant bower she had so lately quitted, and their faces turned towards each other, like little moons under the great white ones which hovered high over the Blue Ridge; his arm dropped softly about her yielding shoulder.

'Well?' he whispered.

'Well.'

Two Wrongs

[1930]

I

'Look at those shoes,' said Bill – 'twenty-eight dollars.'

Mr Brancusi looked. 'Purty.'

'Made to order.'

'I knew you were a great swell. You didn't get me up here to show me those shoes, did you?'

'I am not a great swell. Who said I was a great swell?' demanded Bill. 'Just because I've got more education than most people in show business.'

'And then, you know, you're a handsome young fellow,' said Brancusi dryly.

'Sure I am – compared to you anyhow. The girls think I must be an actor, till they find out.... Got a cigarette? What's more, I look like a man – which is more than some of these pretty boys round Times Square do.'

'Good-looking. Gentleman. Good shoes. Shot with luck.'

'You're wrong there,' objected Bill. 'Brains. Three years – nine shows – four big hits – only one flop. Where do you see any luck in that?'

A little bored, Brancusi just gazed. What he would have seen – had he not made his eyes opaque and taken to thinking about something else – was a fresh-faced young Irishman exuding aggressiveness and self-confidence until the air of his office was thick with it. Presently, Brancusi knew, Bill would hear the sound of his own voice and be ashamed and retire into his other humour – the quietly superior, sensitive one, the patron of the arts, modelled on the intellectuals of the Theatre Guild. Bill McChesney had not quite decided between the two, such blends are seldom complete before thirty.

'Take Ames, take Hopkins, take Harris – take any of them,'

Bill insisted. 'What have they got on me? What's the matter? Do you want a drink?' – seeing Brancusi's glance wander towards the cabinet on the opposite wall.

'I never drink in the morning. I just wondered who it was keeps on knocking. You ought to make it stop. I get a nervous fidgets, kind of half crazy, with that kind of thing.'

Bill went quickly to the door and threw it open.

'Nobody,' he said. . . . 'Hello! What do you want?'

'Oh, I'm so sorry,' a voice answered; 'I'm terribly sorry. I got so excited and I didn't realize I had this pencil in my hand.'

'What is it you want?'

'I want to see you, and the clerk said you were busy. I have a letter for you from Alan Rogers, the playwright – and I wanted to give it to you personally.'

'I'm busy,' said Bill. 'See Mr Cadorna.'

'I did, but he wasn't very encouraging, and Mr Rogers said –'

Brancusi, edging over restlessly, took a quick look at her. She was very young, with beautiful red hair, and more character in her face than her chatter would indicate; it did not occur to Mr Brancusi that this was due to her origin in Delaney, South Carolina.

'What shall I do?' she inquired, quietly laying her future in Bill's hands. 'I had a letter to Mr Rogers, and he just gave me this one to you.'

'Well, what do you want me to do – marry you?' exploded Bill.

'I'd like to get a part in one of your plays.'

'Then sit down and wait. I'm busy. . . . Where's Miss Cohalan?' He rang a bell, looked once more, crossly, at the girl and closed the door of his office. But during the interruption his other mood had come over him, and he resumed his conversation with Brancusi in the key of one who was hand in glove with Reinhardt for the artistic future of the theatre.

By 12.30 he had forgotten everything except that he was going to be the greatest producer in the world and that he had an engagement to tell Sol Lincoln about it at lunch. Emerging from his office, he looked expectantly at Miss Cohalan.

'Mr Lincoln won't be able to meet you,' she said. 'He jus' 'is minute called.'

'Just this minute,' repeated Bill, shocked. 'All right. Just cross him off that list for Thursday night.'

Miss Cohalan drew a line on a sheet of paper before her.

'Mr McChesney, now you haven't forgotten me, have you?'

He turned to the red-headed girl.

'No,' he said vaguely, and then to Miss Cohalan: 'That's all right: ask him for Thursday anyhow. To hell with him!'

He did not want to lunch alone. He did not like to do anything alone now, because contacts were too much fun when one had prominence and power.

'If you would just let me talk to you two minutes —' she began.

'Afraid I can't now.' Suddenly he realized that she was the most beautiful person he had ever seen in his life.

He stared at her.

'Mr Rogers told me —'

'Come and have a spot of lunch with me,' he said, and then, with an air of great hurry, he gave Miss Cohalan some quick and contradictory instructions and held open the door.

They stood on Forty-second Street and he breathed his pre-empted air — there is only enough air there for a few people at a time. It was November and the first exhilarating rush of the season was over, but he could look east and see the electric sign of one of his plays, and west and see another. Around the corner was the one he had put on with Brancusi — the last time he would produce anything except alone.

They went to the Bedford, where there was a to-do of waiters and captains as he came in.

'This is ver' tractive restaurant,' she said, impressed and on company behaviour.

'This is hams' paradise.' He nodded to several people. 'Hello, Jimmy — Bill.... Hello there, Jack....That's Jack Dempsey.... I don't eat here much. I usually eat up at the Harvard Club.'

'Oh, did you go to Harvard? I used to know —'

'Yes.' He hesitated; there were two versions about Harvard, and he decided suddenly on the true one. 'Yes, and they had me down for a hick there, but not any more. About a week ago I was out on Long Island at the Gouverneer Haights – very fashionable people – and a couple of Gold Coast boys that never knew I was alive up in Cambridge began pulling this "Hello, Bill, old boy" on me.'

He hesitated and suddenly decided to leave the story there.

'What do you want – a job?' he demanded. He remembered suddenly that she had holes in her stockings. Holes in stockings always moved him, softened him.

'Yes, or else I've got to go home,' she said. 'I want to be a dancer – you know, Russian Ballet. But the lessons cost so much, so I've got to get a job. I thought it'd give me stage presence anyhow.'

'Hoofer, eh?'

'Oh, no, serious.'

'Well, Pavlova's a hoofer, isn't she?'

'Oh, no.' She was shocked at this profanity, but after a moment she continued: 'I took with Miss Campbell – Georgia Berriman Campbell – back home – maybe you know her. She took from New Wayburn, and she's really wonderful. She –'

'Yeah?' he said abstractedly. 'Well, it's a tough business – casting agencies bursting with people that can all do anything, till I give them a try. How old are you?'

'Eighteen.'

'I'm twenty-six. Came here four years ago without a cent.'

'My!'

'I could quit now and be comfortable the rest of my life.'

'My!'

'Going to take a year off next year – get married. . . . Ever hear of Irene Rikker?'

'I should say! She's about my favourite of all.'

'We're engaged.'

'My!'

When they went out into Times Square after a while he said carelessly, 'What are you doing now?'

'Why, I'm trying to get a job.'

'I mean right this minute.'

'Why, nothing.'

'Do you want to come up to my apartment on Forty-sixth Street and have some coffee?'

Their eyes met, and Emmy Pinkard made up her mind she could take care of herself.

It was a great bright studio apartment with a ten-foot divan, and after she had coffee and he a highball, his arm dropped round her shoulder.

'Why should I kiss you?' she demanded. 'I hardly know you, and besides, you're engaged to somebody else.'

'Oh, that! She doesn't care.'

'No, really!'

'You're a good girl.'

'Well, I'm certainly not an idiot.'

'All right, go on being a good girl.'

She stood up, but lingered a minute, very fresh and cool, and not upset at all.

'I suppose this means you won't give me a job?' she asked pleasantly.

He was already thinking about something else – about an interview and a rehearsal – but now he looked at her again and saw that she still had holes in her stockings. He telephoned:

'Joe, this is the Fresh Boy.... You didn't think I knew you called me that, did you?... It's all right.... Say, have you got those three girls for the party scene? Well, listen; save one for a Southern kid I'm sending around today.'

He looked at her jauntily, conscious of being such a good fellow.

'Well, I don't know how to thank you. And Mr Rogers,' she added audaciously. 'Good-bye, Mr McChesney.'

2

During rehearsal he used to come around a great deal and stand watching with a wise expression, as if he knew everything in people's minds; but actually he was in a haze about his own good fortune and didn't see much and didn't for the moment care. He spent most of his week-ends on Long Island with the fashionable people who had 'taken him up'. When Brancusi referred to him as the 'big social butterfly', he would answer, 'Well, what about it? Didn't I go to Harvard? You think they found me in a Grand Street apple-cart, like you?' He was well liked among his new friends for his good looks and good nature, as well as his success.

His engagement to Irene Rikker was the most unsatisfactory thing in his life; they were tired of each other but unwilling to put an end to it. Just as, often, the two richest young people in a town are drawn together by the fact, so Bill McChesney and Irene Rikker, borne side by side on waves of triumph, could not spare each other's nice appreciation of what was due such success. Nevertheless, they indulged in fiercer and more frequent quarrels, and the end was approaching. It was embodied in one Frank Llewellen, a big, fine-looking actor playing opposite Irene. Seeing the situation at once, Bill became bitterly humorous about it; from the second week of rehearsals there was tension in the air.

Meanwhile Emmy Pinkard, with enough money for crackers and milk, and a friend who took her out to dinner, was being happy. Her friend, Easton Hughes from Delaney, was studying at Columbia to be a dentist. He sometimes brought along other lonesome young men studying to be dentists, and at the price, if it can be called that, of a few casual kisses in taxicabs, Emmy dined when hungry. One afternoon she introduced Easton to Bill McChesney at the stage door, and afterwards Bill made his facetious jealousy the basis of their relationship.

'I see that dental number has been slipping it over on me again. Well, don't let him give you any laughing gas is my advice.'

Though their encounters were few, they always looked at each other. When Bill looked at her he stared for an instant as if he had not seen her before, and then remembered suddenly that she was to be teased. When she looked at him she saw many things – a bright day outside, with great crowds of people hurrying through the streets; a very good new limousine that waited at the kerb for two people with very good new clothes, who got in and went somewhere that was just like New York, only away, and more fun there. Many times she had wished she had kissed him, but just as many times she was glad she hadn't; since, as the weeks passed, he grew less romantic, tied up, like the rest of them, to the play's laborious evolution.

They were opening in Atlantic City. A sudden moodiness, apparent to everyone, came over Bill. He was short with the director and sarcastic with the actors. This, it was rumoured, was because Irene Rikker had come down with Frank Llewellen on a different train. Sitting beside the author on the night of the dress rehearsal, he was an almost sinister figure in the twilight of the auditorium; but he said nothing until the end of the second act, when, with Llewellen and Irene Rikker on the stage alone, he suddenly called:

'We'll go over that again – and cut out the mush!'

Llewellen came down to the footlights.

'What do you mean – cut out the mush?' he inquired. 'Those are the lines, aren't they?'

'You know what I mean – stick to business.'

'I don't know what you mean.'

Bill stood up. 'I mean all that damn whispering.'

'There wasn't any whispering. I simply asked –'

'That'll do – take it over.'

Llewellen turned away furiously and was about to proceed, when Bill added audibly: 'Even a ham has got to do his stuff.'

Llewellen whipped about. 'I don't have to stand that kind of talk, Mr McChesney.'

'Why not? You're a ham, aren't you? When did you get ashamed of being a ham? I'm putting on this play and I want you to stick to your stuff.' Bill got up and walked down the aisle. 'And when you don't do it, I'm going to call you just like anybody else.'

'Well, you watch out for your tone of voice –'

'What'll you do about it?'

Llewellen jumped down into the orchestra pit.

'I'm not taking anything from you!' he shouted.

Irene Rikker called to them from the stage 'For heaven's sake, are you two crazy?' And then Llewellen swung at him, one short, mighty blow. Bill pitched back across a row of seats, fell through one, splintering it, and lay wedged there. There was a moment's wild confusion, then people holding Llewellen, then the author, with a white face, pulling Bill up and the stage manager crying: 'Shall I kill him, chief? Shall I break his fat face?' and Llewellen panting and Irene Rikker frightened.

'Get back there!' Bill cried, holding a handkerchief to his face and teetering into the author's supporting arms. 'Everybody get back! Take that scene again, and no talk! Get back, Llewellen!'

Before they realized it they were all back on the stage, Irene pulling Llewellen's arm and talking to him fast. Someone put on the auditorium lights and then dimmed them again hurriedly. When Emmy came out presently for her scene, she saw in a quick glance that Bill was sitting with a whole mask of handkerchiefs over his bleeding face. She hated Llewellen and was afraid that presently they would break up and go back to New York. But Bill had saved the show from his own folly, since for Llewellen to take the further initiative of quitting would hurt his professional standing. The act ended and the next one began without an interval. When it was over, Bill was gone.

Next night, during the performance, he sat on a chair in the wings in view of everyone coming on or off. His face was swollen and bruised, but he neglected to seem conscious of the fact and there were no comments. Once he went around in front, and when he returned, word leaked out that two of the New York agencies were making big buys. He had a hit – they all had a hit.

At the sight of him to whom Emmy felt they all owed so much, a great wave of gratitude swept over her. She went up and thanked him.

'I'm a good picker, red-head,' he agreed grimly.

'Thank you for picking me.'

And suddenly Emmy was moved to a rash remark.

'You've hurt your face so badly!' she exclaimed. 'Oh, I think it was so brave of you not to let everything go to pieces last night.'

He looked at her hard for a moment and then an ironic smile tried unsuccessfully to settle on his swollen face.

'Do you admire me, baby?'

'Yes.'

'Even when I fell in the seats, did you admire me?'

'You got control of everything so quick.'

'That's loyalty for you. You found something to admire in that fool mess.'

And her happiness bubbled up into, 'Anyhow, you behaved just wonderfully.' She looked so fresh and young that Bill, who had had a wretched day, wanted to rest his swollen cheek against her cheek.

He took both the bruise and the desire with him to New York next morning; the bruise faded, but the desire remained. And when they opened in the city, no sooner did he see other men begin to crowd around her beauty than she became this play for him, this success, the thing that he came to see when he came to the theatre. After a good run it closed just as he was drinking too much and needed someone on the grey days of reaction. They were married suddenly in Connecticut, early in June.

3

Two men sat in the Savoy Grill in London, waiting for the Fourth of July. It was already late in May.

'Is he a nice guy?' asked Hubbel.

'Very nice,' answered Brancusi; 'very nice, very handsome, very popular.' After a moment, he added: 'I want to get him to come home.'

'That's what I don't get about him,' said Hubbel. 'Show

business over here is nothing compared to home. What does he want to stay here for?'

'He goes around with a lot of dukes and ladies.'

'Oh?'

'Last week when I met him he was with three ladies – Lady this, Lady that, Lady the other thing.'

'I thought he was married.'

'Married three years,' said Brancusi, 'got a fine child, going to have another.'

He broke off as McChesney came in, his very American face staring about boldly over the collar of a box-shouldered topcoat.

'Hello, Mac; meet my friend Mr Hubbel.'

'J'doo,' said Bill. He sat down, continuing to stare around the bar to see who was present. After a few minutes Hubbel left, and Bill asked:

'Who's that bird?'

'He's only been here a month. He ain't got a title yet. You been here six months, remember.'

Bill grinned.

'You think I'm high-hat, don't you? Well, I'm not kidding myself anyhow. I like it; it gets me. I'd like to be the Marquis of McChesney.'

'Maybe you can drink yourself into it,' suggested Brancusi.

'Shut your trap. Who said I was drinking? Is that what they say now? Look here; if you can tell me any American manager in the history of the theatre who's had the success that I've had in London in less than eight months, I'll go back to America with you tomorrow. If you'll just tell me –'

'It was with your old shows. You had two flops in New York.'

Bill stood up, his face hardening.

'Who do you think you are?' he demanded. 'Did you come over here to talk to me like that?'

'Don't get sore now, Bill. I just want you to come back. I'd say anything for that. Put over three seasons like you had in '22 and '23, and you're fixed for life.'

'New York makes me sick,' said Bill moodily. 'One minute you're a king; then you have two flops, they go around saying you're on the toboggan.'

Brancusi shook his head.

'That wasn't why they said it. It was because you had that quarrel with Aronstael, your best friend.'

'Friend hell!'

'Your best friend in business anyhow. Then —'

'I don't want to talk about it.' He looked at his watch. 'Look here; Emmy's feeling bad so I'm afraid I can't have dinner with you tonight. Come around to the office before you sail.'

Five minutes later, standing by the cigar counter, Brancusi saw Bill enter the Savoy again and descend the steps that led to the tea room.

'Grown to be a great diplomat,' thought Brancusi; 'he used to just say when he had a date. Going with these dukes and ladies is polishing him up even more.'

Perhaps he was a little hurt, though it was not typical of him to be hurt. At any rate he made a decision, then and there, that McChesney was on the down-grade; it was quite typical of him that at that point he erased him from his mind forever.

There was no outward indication that Bill was on the down-grade; a hit at the New Strand, a hit at the Prince of Wales, and the weekly grosses pouring in almost as well as they had two or three years before in New York. Certainly a man of action was justified in changing his base. And the man who, an hour later, turned into his Hyde Park house for dinner had all the vitality of the late twenties. Emmy, very tired and clumsy, lay on a couch in the upstairs sitting-room. He held her for a moment in his arms.

'Almost over now,' he said. 'You're beautiful.'

'Don't be ridiculous.'

'It's true. You're always beautiful. I don't know why. Perhaps because you've got character, and that's always in your face, even when you're like this.'

She was pleased; she ran her hand through his hair.

'Character is the greatest thing in the world,' he declared, 'and you've got more than anybody I know.'

'Did you see Brancusi?'

'I did, the little louse! I decided not to bring him home to dinner.'

'What was the matter?'

'Oh, just snooty – talking about my row with Aronstael, as if it was my fault.'

She hesitated, closed her mouth tight and then said quietly, 'You got into that fight with Aronstael because you were drinking.'

He rose impatiently.

'Are you going to start –'

'No, Bill, but you're drinking too much now. You know you are.'

Aware that she was right, he evaded the matter and they went into dinner. On the glow of a bottle of claret he decided he would go on the wagon tomorrow till after the baby was born.

'I always stop when I want, don't I? I always do what I say. You never saw me quit yet.'

'Never yet.'

They had coffee together, and afterwards he got up.

'Come back early,' said Emmy.

'Oh, sure. . . . What's the matter, baby?'

'I'm just crying. Don't mind me. Oh, go on; don't just stand there like a big idiot.'

'But I'm worried, naturally. I don't like to see you cry.'

'Oh, I don't know where you go in the evenings; I don't know who you're with. And that Lady Sybil Combrinck who kept phoning. It's all right, I suppose, but I wake up in the night and I feel so alone, Bill. Because we've always been together, haven't we, until recently?'

'But we're together still. . . . What's happened to you, Emmy?'

'I know – I'm just crazy. We'd never let each other down, would we? We never have –'

'Of course not.'

'Come back early, or when you can.'

He looked in for a minute at the Prince of Wales Theatre; then he went into the hotel next door and called a number.

'I'd like to speak to her Ladyship. Mr McChesney calling.'

It was some time before Lady Sybil answered:

'This is rather a surprise. It's been several weeks since I've been lucky enough to hear from you.'

Her voice was flip as a whip and cold as automatic refrigeration, in the mode grown familiar since British ladies took to piecing themselves together out of literature. It had fascinated Bill for a while, but just for a while. He had kept his head.

'I haven't had a minute,' he explained easily. 'You're not sore, are you?'

'I could scarcely say "sore".'

'I was afraid you might be; you didn't send me an invitation to your party tonight. My idea was that after we talked it all over we agreed –'

'You talked a great deal,' she said; 'possibly a little too much.'

Suddenly, to Bill's astonishment, she hung up.

'Going British on me,' he thought. 'A little skit entitled The Daughter of a Thousand Earls.'

The snub roused him, the indifference revived his waning interest. Usually women forgave his changes of heart because of his obvious devotion to Emmy, and he was remembered by various ladies with a not unpleasant sigh. But he had detected no such sigh upon the phone.

'I'd like to clear up this mess,' he thought. Had he been wearing evening clothes, he might have dropped in at the dance and talked it over with her, still he didn't want to go home. Upon consideration it seemed important that the misunderstanding should be fixed up at once, and presently he began to entertain the idea of going as he was; Americans were excused unconventionalities of dress. In any case, it was not nearly time, and, in the company of several highballs, he considered the matter for an hour.

At midnight he walked up the steps of her Mayfair house.

Two Wrongs

The coat-room attendants scrutinized his tweeds disapprovingly and a footman peered in vain for his name on the list of guests. Fortunately his friend Sir Humphrey Dunn arrived at the same time and convinced the footman it must be a mistake.

Inside, Bill immediately looked about for his hostess.

She was a very tall young woman, half American and all the more intensely English. In a sense, she had discovered Bill McChesney, vouched for his savage charms; his retirement was one of her most humiliating experiences since she had begun being bad.

She stood with her husband at the head of the receiving line – Bill had never seen them together before. He decided to choose a less formal moment for presenting himself.

As the receiving went on interminably, he became increasingly uncomfortable. He saw a few people he knew, but not many, and he was conscious that his clothes were attracting a certain attention; he was aware also that Lady Sybil saw him and could have relieved his embarrassment with a wave of her hand, but she made no sign. He was sorry he had come, but to withdraw now would be absurd, and going to a buffet table, he took a glass of champagne.

When he turned around she was alone at last, and he was about to approach her when the butler spoke to him:

'Pardon me, sir. Have you a card?'

'I'm a friend of Lady Sybil's,' said Bill impatiently. He turned away, but the butler followed.

'I'm sorry, sir, but I'll have to ask you to step aside with me and straighten this up.'

'There's no need. I'm just about to speak to Lady Sybil now.'

'My orders are different sir,' said the butler firmly.

Then, before Bill realized what was happening, his arms were pressed quietly to his sides and he was propelled into a little ante-room back of the buffet.

There he faced a man in a pince-nez in whom he recognized the Combrincks' private secretary.

The secretary nodded to the butler, saying, 'This is the man'; whereupon Bill was released.

'Mr McChesney,' said the secretary, 'you have seen fit to force your way here without a card, and His Lordship requests that you leave his house at once. Will you kindly give me the check for your coat?'

Then Bill understood, and the single word that he found applicable to Lady Sybil sprang to his lips; whereupon the secretary gave a sign to two footmen, and in a furious struggle Bill was carried through a pantry where busy bus boys stared at the scene, down a long hall, and pushed out a door into the night. The door closed; a moment later it was opened again to let his coat billow forth and his cane clatter down the steps.

As he stood there, overwhelmed, stricken aghast, a taxi-cab stopped beside him and the driver called:

'Feeling ill, gov'nor?'

'What?'

'I know where you can get a good pick-me-up, gov'nor. Never too late.' The door of the taxi opened on a nightmare. There was a cabaret that broke the closing hours; there was being with strangers he had picked up somewhere; then there were arguments, and trying to cash a cheque, and suddenly proclaiming over and over that he was William McChesney, the producer, and convincing no one of the fact, not even himself. It seemed important to see Lady Sybil right away and call her to account; but presently nothing was important at all. He was in a taxi-cab whose driver had just shaken him awake in front of his own home.

The telephone was ringing as he went in, but he walked stonily past the maid and only heard her voice when his foot was on the stair.

'Mr McChesney, it's the hospital calling again. Mrs McChesney's there, and they've been phoning every hour.'

Still in a daze, he held the receiver up to his ear.

'We're calling from the Midland Hospital, for your wife. She was delivered of a still-born child at nine this morning.'

'Wait a minute.' His voice was dry and cracking. 'I don't understand.'

After a while he understood that Emmy's child was dead and

she wanted him. His knees sagged groggily as he walked down the street, looking for a taxi.

The room was dark; Emmy looked up and saw him from a rumpled bed.

'It's you!' she cried. 'I thought you were dead! Where did you go?'

He threw himself down on his knees beside the bed, but she turned away.

'Oh, you smell awful,' she said. 'It makes me sick.'

But she kept her hand in his hair, and he knelt there motionless for a long time.

'I'm done with you,' she muttered, 'but it was awful when I thought you were dead. Everybody's dead. I wish I was dead.'

A curtain parted with the wind, and as he rose to arrange it, she saw him in the full morning light, pale and terrible, with rumpled clothes and bruises on his face. This time she hated him instead of those who had hurt him. She could feel him slipping out of her heart, feel the space he left, and all at once he was gone, and she could even forgive him and be sorry for him. All this in a minute.

She had fallen down at the door of the hospital, trying to get out of the taxi-cab alone.

4

When Emmy was well, physically and mentally, her incessant idea was to learn to dance; the old dream inculcated by Miss Georgia Berriman Campbell of South Carolina persisted as a bright avenue leading back to first youth and days of hope in New York. To her, dancing meant that elaborate blend of tortuous attitudes and formal pirouettes that evolved out of Italy several hundred years ago and reached its apogee in Russia at the beginning of this century. She wanted to use herself on something she could believe in, and it seemed to her that the dance was woman's interpretation of music; instead of strong fingers, one had limbs with which to render Tschaikowsky and Stravinski; and feet could be as eloquent in Chopiniana as voices in 'The Ring'. At the bottom, it was something sand-wiched in between the acrobats and the trained seals; at the top it was Pavlova and art.

Once they were settled in an apartment back in New York, she plunged into her work like a girl of sixteen – four hours a day at bar exercises, attitudes, sauts, arabesques, and pirou-ettes. It became the realest part of her life, and her only worry was whether or not she was too old. At twenty-six she had ten years to make up, but she was a natural dancer with a fine body – and that lovely face.

Bill encouraged it; when she was ready he was going to build the first real American ballet around her. There were even times when he envied her her absorption; for affairs in his own line were more difficult since they had come home. For one thing, he had made enemies in those early days of self-confidence; there were exaggerated stories of his drinking and of his being hard on actors and difficult to work with.

It was against him that he had always been unable to save money and must beg a backing for each play. Then, too, in a curious way, he was intelligent, as he was brave enough to prove in several uncommercial ventures, but he had no Theatre Guild behind him, and what money he lost was charged against him.

There were successes, too, but he worked harder for them, or it seemed so, for he had begun to pay a price for his irregular life. He always intended to take a rest or give up his incessant cigarettes, but there was so much competition now – new men coming up, with new reputations for infallibility – and besides, he wasn't used to regularity. He liked to do his work in those great spurts, inspired by black coffee, that seem so inevitable in show business, but which took so much out of a man after thirty. He had come to lean, in a way, on Emmy's fine health and vitality. They were always together, and if he felt a vague dissatisfaction that he had grown to need her more than she needed him, there was always the hope that things would break better for him next month, next season.

Coming home from ballet school one November evening,

Two Wrongs

Emmy swung her little grey bag, pulled her hat far down over her still damp hair, and gave herself up to pleasant speculation. For a month she had been aware of people who had come to the studio especially to watch her – she was ready to dance. Once she had worked just as hard and for as long a time on something else – her relations with Bill – only to reach a climax and misery, but here there was nothing to fail her except herself. Yet even now she felt a little rash in thinking: 'Now it's come. I'm going to be happy.'

She hurried, for something had come up today that she must talk over with Bill.

Finding him in the living-room, she called him to come back while she dressed. She began to talk without looking around:

'Listen what happened!' Her voice was loud, to compete with the water running in the tub. 'Paul Makova wants me to dance with him at the Metropolitan this season; only it's not sure, so it's a secret – even I'm not supposed to know.'

'That's great.'

'The only thing is whether it wouldn't be far better for me to make a début abroad? Anyhow Donilof says I'm ready to appear. What do you think?'

'I don't know.'

'You don't sound very enthusiastic.'

'I've got something on my mind. I'll tell you about it later. Go on.'

'That's all, dear. If you still feel like going to Germany for a month, like you said, Donilof would arrange a début for me in Berlin, but I'd rather open here and dance with Paul Makova. Just imagine –' She broke off, feeling suddenly through the thick skin of her elation how abstracted he was. 'Tell me what you've got on your mind.'

'I went to Doctor Kearns this afternoon.'

'What did he say?' Her mind was still singing with her own happiness. Bill's intermittent attacks of hypochondria had long ceased to worry her.

'I told him about that blood this morning, and he said what he said last year – it was probably a little broken vein in my throat. But since I'd been coughing and was worried, perhaps it was safer to take an X-ray and clear the matter up. Well, we cleared it up all right. My left lung is practically gone.

'Bill!'

'Luckily there are no spots on the other.'

She waited, horribly afraid.

'It's come at a bad time for me,' he went on steadily, 'but it's got to be faced. He thinks I ought to go to the Adirondacks or to Denver for the winter, and his idea is Denver. That way it'll probably clear up in five or six months.'

'Of course we'll have to –' she stopped suddenly.

'I wouldn't expect you to go – especially if you have this opportunity.'

'Of course I'll go,' she said quickly. 'Your health comes first. We've always gone everywhere together.'

'Oh, no.'

'Why, of course.' She made her voice strong and decisive. 'We've always been together. I couldn't stay here without you. When do you have to go?'

'As soon as possible. I went in to see Brancusi to find out if he wanted to take over the Richmond piece, but he didn't seem enthusiastic.' His face hardened. 'Of course there won't be any-thing else for the present, but I'll have enough, with what's owing –'

'Oh, if I was only making some money!' Emmy cried. 'You work so hard and here I've been spending two hundred dollars a week for just my dancing lessons alone – more than I'll be able to earn for years.'

'Of course in six months I'll be as well as ever – he says.'

'Sure, dearest; we'll get you well. We'll start as soon as we can.'

She put an arm around him and kissed him.

'I'm just an old parasite,' she said. 'I should have known my darling wasn't well.'

He reached automatically for a cigarette, and then stopped.

'I forgot – I've got to start cutting down smoking.' He rose to the occasion suddenly: 'No, baby, I've decided to go alone. You'd go crazy with boredom out there, and I'd just be thinking I was keeping you away from your dancing.'

'Don't think about that. The thing is to get you well.'

They discussed the matter hour after hour for the next week, each of them saying everything except the truth – that he wanted her to go with him and that she wanted passionately to stay in New York. She talked it over guardedly with Donilof, her ballet master, and found that he thought any postponement would be a terrible mistake. Seeing other girls in the ballet school making plans for the winter, she wanted to die rather than go, and Bill saw all the involuntary indications of her misery. For a while they talked of compromising on the Adirondacks, whither she would commute by aeroplane for the weekends, but he was running a little fever now and he was definitely ordered West.

Bill settled it all one gloomy Sunday night, with that rough, generous justice that had first made her admire him, that made him rather tragic in his adversity, as he had always been bearable in his overweening success:

'It's just up to me, baby. I got into this mess because I didn't have any self-control – you seem to have all of that in this family – and now it's only me that can get me out. You've worked hard at your stuff for three years and you deserve your chance – and if you came out there now you'd have it on me the rest of my life.' He grinned. 'And I couldn't stand that. Besides, it wouldn't be good for the kid.'

Eventually she gave in, ashamed of herself, miserable – and glad. For the world of her work, where she existed without Bill, was bigger to her now than the world in which they existed together. There was more room to be glad in one than to be sorry in the other.

Two days later, with his ticket bought for that afternoon at five, they passed the last hours together, talking of everything hopeful. She protested still, and sincerely; had he weakened for a moment she would have gone. But the shock had done something to him, and he showed more character under it than he had for years. Perhaps it would be good for him to work it out alone.

'In the spring!' they said.

Then in the station with little Billy, and Bill saying: 'I hate these graveside partings. You leave me here. I've got to make a phone call from the train before it goes.'

They had never spent more than a night apart in six years, save when Emmy was in the hospital; save for the time in England they had a good record of faithfulness and of tenderness towards each other, even though she had been alarmed and often unhappy at this insecure bravado from the first. After he went through the gate alone, Emmy was glad he had a phone call to make and tried to picture him making it.

She was a good woman; she had loved him with all her heart. When she went out into Thirty-third Street, it was just as dead as dead for a while, and the apartment he paid for would be empty of him, and she was here, about to do something that would make her happy.

She stopped after a few blocks, thinking: 'Why, this is terrible – what I'm doing! I'm letting him down like the worst person I ever heard of. I'm leaving him flat and going off to dinner with Donilof and Paul Makova, whom I like for being beautiful and for having the same colour eyes and hair. Bill's on the train alone.'

She swung little Billy around suddenly as if to go back to the station. She could see him sitting in the train, with his face so pale and tired, and no Emmy.

'I can't let him down,' she cried to herself as wave after wave of sentiment washed over her. But only sentiment – hadn't he let her down – hadn't he done what he wanted in London?

'Oh, poor Bill!'

She stood irresolute, realizing for the last honest moment how quickly she would forget this and find excuses for what she was doing. She had to think hard of London, and her conscience cleared. But with Bill all alone in the train it seemed terrible to think that way. Even now she could turn and go back to the station and tell him that she was coming, but she still waited, with life very strong in her, fighting for her. The sidewalk was narrow where she stood; presently a great wave of people, pouring out of the theatre, came flooding along it, and she and little Billy were swept along with the crowd.

In the train, Bill telephoned up to the last minute, postponed going back to his state-room, because he knew it was almost certain that he would not find her there. After the train started he went back and, of course, there was nothing but his bags in the rack and some magazines on the seat.

He knew then that he had lost her. He saw the set-up without any illusions – this Paul Makova, and months of proximity, and loneliness – afterwards nothing would ever be the same. When he had thought about it all a long time, reading *Variety* and *Zit's* in between, it began to seem, each time he came back to it, as if Emmy somehow were dead.

'She was a fine girl – one of the best. She had character.' He realized perfectly that he had brought all this on himself and that there was some law of compensation involved. He saw, too, that by going away he had again become as good as she was; it was all evened up at last.

He felt beyond everything, even beyond his grief, an almost comfortable sensation of being in the hands of something bigger than himself; and grown a little tired and unconfident – two qualities he could never for a moment tolerate – it did not seem so terrible if he were going West for a definite finish. He was sure that Emmy would come at the end, no matter what she was doing or how good an engagement she had.

The Bridal Party

[1930]

I

There was the usual insincere little note saying: 'I wanted you to be the first to know.' It was a double shock to Michael, announcing, as it did, both the engagement and the imminent marriage; which, moreover, was to be held, not in New York, decently and far away, but here in Paris under his very nose, if that could be said to extend over the Protestant Episcopal Church of the Holy Trinity, Avenue Georges-Cinq. The date was two weeks off, early in June.

At first Michael was afraid and his stomach felt hollow. When he left the hotel that morning, the *femme de chambre*, who was in love with his fine, sharp profile and his pleasant buoyancy, scented the hard abstraction that had settled over him. He walked in a daze to his bank, he bought a detective story at Smith's on the Rue de Rivoli, he sympathetically stared for a while at a faded panorama of the battlefields in a tourist-office window and cursed a Greek tout who followed him with a half-displayed packet of innocuous post cards warranted to be very dirty indeed.

But the fear stayed with him, and after a while he recognized it as the fear that now he would never be happy. He had met Caroline Dandy when she was seventeen, possessed her young heart all through her first season in New York, and then lost her, slowly, tragically, uselessly, because he had no money and could make no money; because, with all the energy and good-will in the world, he could not find himself; because, loving him still, Caroline had lost faith and begun to see him as something pathetic, futile, and shabby, outside the great, shining stream of life towards which she was inevitably drawn.

Since his only support was that she loved him, he leaned

75

weakly on that; the support broke, but still he held on to it and was carried out to sea and washed up on the French coast with its broken pieces still in his hands. He carried them around with him in the form of photographs and packets of correspondence and a liking for a maudlin popular song called 'Among My Souvenirs'. He kept clear of other girls, as if Caroline would somehow know it and reciprocate with a faithful heart. Her note informed him that he had lost her forever.

It was a fine morning. In front of the shops in the Rue de Castiglione, proprietors and patrons were on the sidewalk gazing upward, for the Graf Zeppelin, shining and glorious, symbol of escape and destruction – of escape, if necessary, through destruction – glided in the Paris sky. He heard a woman say in French that it would not astonish her if that commenced to let fall the bombs. Then he heard another voice, full of husky laughter, and the void in his stomach froze. Jerking about, he was face to face with Caroline Dandy and her fiancé.

'Why, Michael! Why, we were wondering where you were. I asked at the Guaranty Trust, and Morgan and Company, and finally sent a note to the National City –'

Why didn't they back away? Why didn't they back right up, walking backwards down the Rue de Castiglione, across the Rue de Rivoli, through the Tuileries Gardens, still walking backwards as fast as they could till they grew vague and faded out across the river?

'This is Hamilton Rutherford, my fiancé.'

'We've met before.'

'At Pat's, wasn't it?'

'And last spring in the Ritz Bar.'

'Michael, where have you been keeping yourself?'

'Around here.' This agony. Previews of Hamilton Rutherford flashed before his eyes – a quick series of pictures, sentences. He remembered hearing that he had bought a seat in 1920 for a hundred and twenty-five thousand of borrowed money, and just before the break sold it for more than half a million. Not handsome like Michael, but vitally attractive, confident, authoritative, just the right height over Caroline there – Michael had always been too short for Caroline when they danced.

Rutherford was saying: 'No, I'd like it very much if you'd come to the bachelor dinner. I'm taking the Ritz Bar from nine o'clock on. Then right after the wedding there'll be a reception and breakfast at the Hôtel Georges-Cinq.'

'And, Michael, George Packman is giving a party day after tomorrow at Chez Victor, and I want you to be sure and come. And also to tea Friday at Jebby West's; she'd want to have you if she knew where you were. Where's your hotel, so we can send you an invitation? You see, the reason we decided to have it over here is because mother has been sick in a nursing home here and the whole clan is in Paris. Then Hamilton's mother's being here too –'

The entire clan; they had always hated him, except her mother; always discouraged his courtship. What a little counter he was in this game of families and money! Under his hat his brow sweated with the humiliation of the fact that for all his misery he was worth just exactly so many invitations. Frantically he began to mumble something about going away.

Then it happened – Caroline saw deep into him, and Michael knew that she saw. She saw through to his profound woundedness, and something quivered inside her, died out along the curve of her mouth and in her eyes. He had moved her. All the unforgettable impulses of first love had surged up once more; their hearts had in some way touched across two feet of Paris sunlight. She took her fiancé's arm suddenly, as if to steady herself with the feel of it.

They parted. Michael walked quickly for a minute; then he stopped, pretending to look in a window, and saw them farther up the street, walking fast into the Place Vendôme, people with much to do.

He had things to do also – he had to get his laundry.

'Nothing will ever be the same again,' he said to himself. 'She will never be happy in her marriage and I will never be happy at all any more.'

The two vivid years of his love for Caroline moved back around him like years in Einstein's physics. Intolerable memories arose – of rides in the Long Island moonlight; of a happy time at Lake Placid with her cheeks so cold there, but warm just underneath the surface; of a despairing afternoon in a little café on Forty-eighth Street in the last sad months when their marriage had come to seem impossible.

'Come in,' he said aloud.

The concierge with a telegram; brusque, because Mr Curly's clothes were a little shabby. Mr Curly gave few tips; Mr Curly was obviously a *petit client*.

Michael read the telegram.

'An answer?' the concierge asked.

'No,' said Michael, and then, on an impulse: 'Look.'

'Too bad – too bad,' said the concierge. 'Your grandfather is dead.'

'Not too bad,' said Michael. 'It means that I come into a quarter of a million dollars.'

Too late by a single month; after the first flush of the news his misery was deeper than ever. Lying awake in bed that night, he listened endlessly to the long caravan of a circus moving through the street from one Paris fair to another.

When the last van had rumbled out of hearing and the corners of the furniture were pastel blue with the dawn, he was still thinking of the look in Caroline's eyes that morning – the look that seemed to say: 'Oh, why couldn't you have done something about it? Why couldn't you have been stronger, made me marry you? Don't you see how sad I am?'

Michael's fists clenched.

'Well, I won't give up till the last moment,' he whispered. 'I've had all the bad luck so far, and maybe it's turned at last. One takes what one can get, up to the limit of one's strength, and if I can't have her, at least she'll go into this marriage with some of me in her heart.'

2

Acordingly he went to the party at Chez Victor two days later, upstairs and into the little salon off the bar where the party was to assemble for cocktails. He was early; the only other occupant was a tall lean man of fifty. They spoke.

'You waiting for George Packman's party?'

'Yes. My name's Michael Curly.'

'My name's –'

Michael failed to catch the name. They ordered a drink, and Michael supposed that the bride and groom were having a gay time.

'Too much so,' the other agreed, frowning. 'I don't see how they stand it. We all crossed on the boat together; five days of that crazy life and then two weeks of Paris. You' – he hesitated, smiling faintly – 'you'll excuse me for saying that your generation drinks too much.'

'Not Caroline.'

'No, not Caroline. She seems to take only a cocktail and a glass of champagne, and then she's had enough, thank God. But Hamilton drinks too much and all this crowd of young people drink too much. Do you live in Paris?'

'For the moment,' said Michael.

'I don't like Paris. My wife – that is to say, my ex-wife, Hamilton's mother – lives in Paris.'

'You're Hamilton Rutherford's father?'

'I have that honour. And I'm not denying that I'm proud of what he's done; it was just a general comment.'

'Of course.'

Michael glanced up nervously as four people came in. He felt suddenly that his dinner coat was old and shiny; he had ordered a new one that morning. The people who had come in were rich and at home in their richness with one another – a dark, lovely girl with a hysterical little laugh whom he had met before; two confident men whose jokes referred invariably to last night's scandal and tonight's potentialities, as if they had important rôles in a play that extended indefinitely into the past and the future. When Caroline arrived, Michael had scarcely a moment of her, but it was enough to note that, like all the others, she was strained and tired. She was pale beneath her rouge; there were shadows under her eyes. With a mixture of relief and wounded vanity, he found himself placed far from her and at another table; he needed a moment to adjust himself to his surroundings. This was not like the immature set in which he and Caroline had moved; the men were more than thirty and had an air of sharing the best of this world's goods. Next to him was Jebby West, whom he knew; and, on the other side, a jovial man who immediately began to talk to Michael about a stunt for the bachelor dinner: They were going to hire a French girl to appear with an actual baby in her arms, crying: 'Hamilton, you can't desert me now!' The idea seemed stale and unamusing to Michael, but its originator shook with anticipatory laughter.

Farther up the table there was talk of the market – another drop today, the most appreciable since the crash; people were kidding Rutherford about it: 'Too bad, old man. You better not get married, after all.'

Michael asked the man on his left, 'Has he lost a lot?'

'Nobody knows. He's heavily involved, but he's one of the smartest young men in Wall Street. Anyhow, nobody ever tells you the truth.'

It was a champagne dinner from the start, and towards the end it reached a pleasant level of conviviality, but Michael saw that all these people were too weary to be exhilarated by any ordinary stimulant; for weeks they had drunk cocktails before meals like Americans, wines and brandies like Frenchmen, beer like Germans, whisky-and-soda like the English, and as they were no longer in the twenties, this preposterous *mélange*, that was like some gigantic cocktail in a nightmare, served only to make them temporarily less conscious of the mistakes of the night before. Which is to say that it was not really a gay party; what gaiety existed was displayed in the few who drank nothing at all.

But Michael was not tired, and the champagne stimulated him and made his misery less acute. He had been away from New York for more than eight months and most of the dance music was unfamiliar to him, but at the first bars of the 'Painted Doll' to which he and Caroline had moved through so much happiness and despair the previous summer, he crossed to Caroline's table and asked her to dance.

She was lovely in a dress of thin ethereal blue, and the proximity of her crackly yellow hair, of her cool and tender grey eyes, turned his body clumsy and rigid; he stumbled with their first step on the floor. For a moment it seemed that there was nothing to say; he wanted to tell her about his inheritance, but the idea seemed abrupt, unprepared for.

'Michael, it's so nice to be dancing with you again.'

He smiled grimly.

'I'm so happy you came,' she continued. 'I was afraid maybe you'd be silly and stay away. Now we can be just good friends and natural together. Michael, I want you and Hamilton to like each other.'

The engagement was making her stupid; he had never heard her make such a series of obvious remarks before.

'I could kill him without a qualm,' he said pleasantly, 'but he looks like a good man. He's fine. What I want to know is, what happens to people like me who aren't able to forget?'

As he said this he could not prevent his mouth from drooping suddenly, and glancing up, Caroline saw, and her heart quivered violently, as it had the other morning.

'Do you mind so much, Michael?'

'Yes.'

For a second as he said this, in a voice that seemed to have come up from his shoes, they were not dancing; they were simply clinging together. Then she leaned away from him and twisted her mouth into a lovely smile.

'I didn't know what to do at first, Michael. I told Hamilton about you – that I'd cared for you an awful lot – but it didn't worry him, and he was right. Because I'm over you now – yes, I am. And you'll wake up some sunny morning and be over me just like that.'

He shook his head stubbornly.

'Oh, yes. We weren't for each other. I'm pretty flighty, and I need somebody like Hamilton to decide things. It was that more than the question of – of –'

'Of money.' Again he was on the point of telling her what had happened, but again something told him it was not the time.

'Then how do you account for what happened when we met the other day,' he demanded helplessly – 'what happened just now? When we just pour towards each other like we used to – as if we were one person, as if the same blood was flowing through both of us?'

'Oh, don't!' she begged him. 'You mustn't talk like that; everything's decided now. I love Hamilton with all my heart. It's just that I remember certain things in the past and I feel sorry for you – for us – for the way we were.'

Over her shoulder, Michael saw a man come towards them to cut in. In a panic he danced her away, but inevitably the man came on.

'I've got to see you alone, if only for a minute,' Michael said quickly. 'When can I?'

'I'll be at Jebby West's tea tomorrow,' she whispered as a hand fell politely upon Michael's shoulder.

But he did not talk to her at Jebby West's tea. Rutherford stood next to her, and each brought the other into all conversations. They left early. The next morning the wedding cards arrived in the first mail.

Then Michael, grown desperate with pacing up and down his room, determined on a bold stroke; he wrote to Hamilton Rutherford, asking him for a rendezvous the following afternoon. In a short telephone communication Rutherford agreed, but for a day later than Michael had asked. And the wedding was only six days away.

They were to meet in the bar of the Hôtel Jéna. Michael knew what he would say: 'See here, Rutherford, do you realize the responsibility you're taking in going through with this marriage? Do you realize the harvest of trouble and regret you're sowing in persuading a girl into something contrary to the instincts of her heart?' He would explain that the barrier between Caroline and himself had been an artificial one and was now removed, and demand that the matter be put up to Caroline frankly before it was too late.

Rutherford would be angry, conceivably there would be a scene, but Michael felt that he was fighting for his life now.

He found Rutherford in conversation with an older man, whom Michael had met at several of the wedding parties.

'I saw what happened to most of my friends,' Rutherford was saying, 'and I decided it wasn't going to happen to mè. It isn't so difficult; if you take a girl with common sense, and tell her what's what, and do your stuff damn well, and play decently square with her, it's a marriage. If you stand for any nonsense at the beginning, it's one of these arrangements – within five years the man gets out, or else the girl gobbles him up and you have the usual mess.'

'Right!' agreed his companion enthusiastically. 'Hamilton, boy, you're right.'

Michael's blood boiled slowly.

'Doesn't it strike you,' he inquired coldly, 'that your attitude went out of fashion about a hundred years ago?'

'No, it didn't,' said Rutherford pleasantly, but impatiently. 'I'm as modern as anybody. I'd get married in an aeroplane next Saturday if it'd please my girl.'

'I don't mean that way of being modern. You can't take a sensitive woman –'

'Sensitive? Women aren't so darn sensitive. It's fellows like you who are sensitive; it's fellows like you that they exploit – all your devotion and kindness and all that. They read a couple of books and see a few pictures because they haven't got anything else to do, and then they say they're finer in grain than you are, and to prove it they take the bit in their teeth and tear off for a fare-you-well – just about as sensitive as a fire horse.'

'Caroline happens to be sensitive,' said Michael in a clipped voice.

At this point the other man got up to go; when the dispute about the check had been settled and they were alone, Rutherford leaned back to Michael as if a question had been asked him.

'Caroline's more than sensitive,' he said. 'She's got sense.'

His combative eyes, meeting Michael's, flickered with a grey light. 'This all sounds pretty crude to you, Mr Curly, but it seems to me that the average man nowadays just asks to be made a monkey of by some woman who doesn't even get any fun out of reducing him to that level. There are darn few men who possess their wives any more, but I am going to be one of them.'

To Michael it seemed time to bring the talk back to the actual situation: 'Do you realize the responsibility you're taking?'

'I certainly do,' interrupted Rutherford. 'I'm not afraid of responsibility. I'll make the decisions – fairly, I hope, but anyhow they'll be final.'

'What if you didn't start right?' said Michael impetuously. 'What if your marriage isn't founded on mutual love?'

'I think I see what you mean,' Rutherford said, still pleasant. 'And since you've brought it up, let me say that if you and Caroline had married, it wouldn't have lasted three years. Do you know what your affair was founded on? On sorrow. You got sorry for each other. Sorrow's a lot of fun for most women and for some men, but it seems to me that a marriage ought to be based on hope.' He looked at his watch and stood up.

'I've got to meet Caroline. Remember, you're coming to the bachelor dinner day after tomorrow.'

Michael felt the moment slipping away. 'Then Caroline's personal feelings don't count with you?' he demanded fiercely.

'Caroline's tired and upset. But she has what she wants, and that's the main thing.'

'Are you referring to yourself?' demanded Michael incredulously.

'Yes.'

'May I ask how long she's wanted you?'

'About two years.' Before Michael could answer, he was gone.

During the next two days Michael floated in an abyss of helplessness. The idea haunted him that he had left something undone that would sever this knot drawn tight under his eyes. He phoned Caroline, but she insisted that it was physically impossible for her to see him until the day before the wedding, for which day she granted him a tentative rendezvous. Then he went to the bachelor dinner, partly in fear of an evening alone at his hotel, partly from a feeling that by his presence at that function he was somehow nearer to Caroline, keeping her in sight.

The Ritz Bar had been prepared for the occasion by French and American banners and by a great canvas covering one wall, against which the guests were invited to concentrate their proclivities in breaking glasses.

At the first cocktail, taken at the bar, there were many slight spillings from many trembling hands, but later, with the champagne, there was a rising tide of laughter and occasional bursts of song.

Michael was surprised to find what a difference his new dinner coat, his new silk hat, his new, proud linen made in his estimate of himself; he felt less resentment towards all these people for being so rich and assured. For the first time since he had left college he felt rich and assured himself; he felt that he was part of all this, and even entered into the scheme of Johnson, the practical joker, for the appearance of the woman betrayed, now waiting tranquilly in the room across the hall.

'We don't want to go too heavy,' Johnson said, 'because I imagine Ham's had a pretty anxious day already. Did you see Fullman Oil's sixteen points off this morning?'

'Will that matter to him?' Michael asked, trying to keep the interest out of his voice.

'Naturally. He's in heavily; he's always in everything heavily. So far he's had luck; anyhow, up to a month ago.'

The glasses were filled and emptied faster now, and men were shouting at one another across the narrow table. Against the bar a group of ushers was being photographed, and the flash light surged through the room in a stifling cloud.

'Now's the time,' Johnson said. 'You're to stand by the door, remember, and we're both to try and keep her from coming in – just till we get everybody's attention.'

He went on out into the corridor, and Michael waited

obediently by the door. Several minutes passed. Then Johnson reappeared with a curious expression on his face.

'There's something funny about this.'

'Isn't the girl there?'

'She's there all right, but there's another woman there, too; and it's nobody we engaged either. She wants to see Hamilton Rutherford, and she looks as if she had something on her mind

They went out into the hall. Planted firmly in a chair near the door sat an American girl a little the worse for liquor, but with a determined expression on her face. She looked up at them with a jerk of her head.

'Well, j'tell him?' she demanded. 'The name is Marjorie Collins, and he'll know it. I've come a long way, and I want to see him now and quick, or there's going to be more trouble than you ever saw.' She rose unsteadily to her feet.

'You go in and tell Ham,' whispered Johnson to Michael. 'Maybe he'd better get out. I'll keep her here.'

Back at the table, Michael leaned close to Rutherford's ear and, with a certain grimness, whispered:

'A girl outside named Marjorie Collins says she wants to see you. She looks as if she wanted to make trouble.'

Hamilton Rutherford blinked and his mouth fell ajar; then slowly the lips came together in a straight line and he said in a crisp voice:

'Please keep her there. And send the head barman to me right away.'

Michael spoke to the barman, and then, without returning to the table, asked quietly for his coat and hat. Out in the hall again, he passed Johnson and the girl without speaking and went out into the Rue Cambon. Calling a cab, he gave the address of Caroline's hotel.

His place was beside her now. Not to bring bad news, but simply to be with her when her house of cards came falling around her head.

Rutherford had implied that he was soft – well, he was hard enough not to give up the girl he loved without taking advantage of every chance within the pale of honour. Should she turn away from Rutherford, she would find him there.

She was in; she was surprised when he called, but she was still dressed and would be down immediately. Presently she appeared in a dinner gown, holding two blue telegrams in her hand. They sat down in armchairs in the deserted lobby.

'But, Michael, is the dinner over?'

'I wanted to see you, so I came away.'

'I'm glad.' Her voice was friendly, but matter-of-fact. 'Because I'd just phoned your hotel that I had fittings and rehearsals all day tomorrow. Now we can have our talk after all.'

'You're tired,' he guessed. 'Perhaps I shouldn't have come.'

'No. I was waiting up for Hamilton. Telegrams that may be important. He said he might go on somewhere, and that may mean any hour, so I'm glad I have someone to talk to.'

Michael winced at the impersonality in the last phrase.

'Don't you care when he gets home?'

'Naturally,' she said, laughing, 'but I haven't got much say about it, have it?'

'Why not?'

'I couldn't start by telling him what he could and couldn't do.'

'Why not?'

'He wouldn't stand for it.'

'He seems to want merely a housekeeper,' said Michael ironically.

'Tell me about your plans, Michael,' she asked quickly.

'My plans? I can't see any future after the day after tomorrow. The only real plan I ever had was to love you.'

Their eyes brushed past each other's, and the look he knew so well was staring out at him from hers. Words flowed quickly from his heart:

'Let me tell you just once more how well I've loved you, never wavering for a moment, never thinking of another girl. And now when I think of all the years ahead without you, without any hope, I don't want to live, Caroline darling. I used to dream about our home, our children, about holding you in my arms and touching your face and hands and hair that used to belong to me, and now I just can't wake up.'

Caroline was crying softly. 'Poor Michael – poor Michael.' Her hand reached out and her fingers brushed the lapel of his dinner coat. 'I was so sorry for you the other night. You looked so thin, and as if you needed a new suit and somebody to take care of you.' She sniffled and looked more closely at his coat. 'Why, you've got a new suit! And a new silk hat! Why, Michael, how swell!' She laughed, suddenly cheerful through her tears. 'You must have come into money, Michael; I never saw you so well turned out.'

For a moment, at her reaction, he hated his new clothes.

'I have come into money,' he said. 'My grandfather left me about a quarter of a million dollars.'

'Why, Michael,' she cried, 'how perfectly swell! I can't tell you how glad I am. I've always thought you were the sort of person who ought to have money.'

'Yes, just too late to make a difference.'

The revolving door from the street groaned around and Hamilton Rutherford came into the lobby. His face was flushed, his eyes were restless and impatient.

'Hello, darling; hello, Mr Curly.' He bent and kissed Caroline. 'I broke away for a minute to find out if I had any telegrams. I see you've got them there.' Taking them from her, he remarked to Curly, 'That was an odd business there in the bar, wasn't it? Especially as I understand some of you had a joke fixed up in the same line.' He opened one of the telegrams, closed it and turned to Caroline with the divided expression of a man carrying two things in his head at once.

'A girl I haven't seen for two years turned up,' he said. 'It seemed to be some clumsy form of blackmail, for I haven't and never have had any sort of obligation towards her whatever.'

'What happened?'

'The head barman had a Sûreté Générale man there in ten minutes and it was settled in the hall. The French blackmail laws make ours look like a sweet wish, and I gather they threw a scare into her that she'll remember. But it seems wiser to tell you.'

'Are you implying that I mentioned the matter?' said Michael stiffly.

'No,' Rutherford said slowly. 'No, you were just going to be on hand. And since you're here, I'll tell you some news that will interest you even more.'

He handed Michael one telegram and opened the other.

'This is in code,' Michael said.

'So is this. But I've got to know all the words pretty well this last week. The two of them together mean I'm due to start life all over.'

Michael saw Caroline's face grow a shade paler, but she sat quiet as a mouse.

'It was a mistake and I stuck to it too long,' continued Rutherford. 'So you see I don't have all the luck, Mr Curly. By the way, they tell me you've come into money.'

'Yes,' said Michael.

'There we are, then.' Rutherford turned to Caroline. 'You understand, darling, that I'm not joking or exaggerating. I've lost almost every cent I had and I'm starting life over.'

Two pairs of eyes were regarding her — Rutherford's non-committal and unrequiring, Michael's hungry, tragic, pleading. In a minute she had raised herself from the chair and with a little cry thrown herself into Hamilton Rutherford's arms.

'Oh, darling,' she cried, 'what does it matter! It's better; I like it better, honestly I do! I want to start that way; I want to! Oh, please don't worry or be sad even for a minute!'

'All right, baby,' said Rutherford. His hand stroked her hair gently for a moment; then he took his arm from around her.

'I promised to join the party for an hour,' he said. 'So I'll say good night, and I want you to go to bed soon and get a good sleep. Good night, Mr Curly. I'm sorry to have let you in for all these financial matters.'

But Michael had already picked up his hat and cane. 'I'll go along with you,' he said.

3

It was such a fine morning. Michael's cutaway hadn't been delivered, so he felt rather uncomfortable passing before the cameras and moving-picture machines in front of the little church on the Avenue Georges-Cinq.

It was such a clean, new church that it seemed unforgivable not to be dressed properly, and Michael, white and shaky after a sleepless night, decided to stand in the rear. From there he looked at the back of Hamilton Rutherford, and the lacy, filmy back of Caroline, and the fat back of George Packman, which looked unsteady, as if it wanted to lean against the bride and groom.

The ceremony went on for a long time under the gay flags and pennons overhead, under the thick beams of June sunlight slanting down through the tall windows upon the well-dressed people.

As the procession, headed by the bride and groom, started down the aisle, Michael realized with alarm he was just where everyone would dispense with the parade stiffness, become informal and speak to him.

So it turned out. Rutherford and Caroline spoke first to him; Rutherford grim with the strain of being married, and Caroline lovelier than he had ever seen her, floating all softly down through the past and forward to the future by the sunlit door.

Michael managed to murmur, 'Beautiful, simply beautiful,' and then other people passed and spoke to him – old Mrs Dandy, straight from her sickbed and looking remarkably well, or carrying it off like the very fine old lady she was; and Rutherford's father and mother, ten years divorced, but walking side by side and looking made for each other and proud. Then all Caroline's sisters and their husbands and her little nephews in Eton suits, and then a long parade, all speaking to Michael because he was still standing paralysed just at that point where the procession broke.

He wondered what would happen now. Cards had been issued

for a reception at the Georges-Cinq; an expensive enough place, heaven knew. Would Rutherford try to go through with that on top of those disastrous telegrams? Evidently, for the procession outside was streaming up there through the June morning, three by three and four by four. On the corner the long dresses of girls, five abreast, fluttered many-coloured in the wind. Girls had become gossamer again, perambulatory flora; such lovely fluttering dresses in the bright noon wind.

Michael needed a drink; he couldn't face that reception line without a drink. Diving into a side doorway of the hotel, he asked for the bar, whither a *chasseur* led him through half a kilometre of new American-looking passages.

But – how did it happen? – the bar was full. There were ten – fifteen men and two – four girls, all from the wedding, all needing a drink. There were cocktails and champagne in the bar; Rutherford's cocktails and champagne, as it turned out, for he had engaged the whole bar and the ballroom and the two great reception rooms and all the stairways leading up and down, and windows looking out over the whole square block of Paris. By and by Michael went and joined the long, slow drift of the receiving line. Through a flowery mist of 'Such a lovely wedding', 'My dear, you were simply lovely', 'You're a lucky man, Rutherford' he passed down the line. When Michael came to Caroline, she took a single step forward and kissed him on the lips, but he felt no contact in the kiss; it was unreal and he floated on away from it. Old Mrs Dandy, who had always liked him, held his hand for a minute and thanked him for the flowers he had sent when he heard she was ill.

'I'm so sorry not to have written; you know, we old ladies are grateful for –' The flowers, the fact that she had not written, the wedding – Michael saw that they all had the same relative importance to her now; she had married off five other children and seen two of the marriages go to pieces, and this scene, so poignant, so confusing to Michael, appeared to her simply a familiar charade in which she had played her part before.

A buffet luncheon with champagne was already being served at small tables and there was an orchestra playing in the empty ballroom. Michael sat down with Jebby West; he was still a little embarrassed at not wearing a morning coat, but he perceived now that he was not alone in the omission and felt better. 'Wasn't Caroline divine?' Jebby West said. 'So entirely self-possessed. I asked her this morning if she wasn't a little nervous at stepping off like this. And she said, "Why should I be? I've been after him for two years, and now I'm just happy, that's all."'

'It must be true,' said Michael gloomily.

'What?'

'What you just said.'

He had been stabbed, but, rather to his distress, he did not feel the wound.

He asked Jebby to dance. Out on the floor, Rutherford's father and mother were dancing together.

'It makes me a little sad, that,' she said. 'Those two hadn't met for years; both of them were married again and she divorced again. She went to the station to meet him when he came over for Caroline's wedding, and invited him to stay at her house in the Avenue du Bois with a whole lot of other people, perfectly proper, but he was afraid his wife would hear about it and not like it, so he went to a hotel. Don't you think that's sort of sad?'

An hour or so later Michael realized suddenly that it was afternoon. In one corner of the ballroom an arrangement of screens like a moving-picture stage had been set up and photographers were taking official pictures of the bridal party. The bridal party, still as death and pale as wax under the bright lights, appeared, to the dancers circling the modulated semi-darkness of the ballroom, like those jovial or sinister groups that one comes upon in The Old Mill at an amusement park.

After the bridal party had been photographed, there was a group of the ushers; then the bridesmaids, the families, the children. Later Caroline, active and excited, having long since abandoned the repose implicit in her flowing dress and great bouquet, came and plucked Michael off the floor.

'Now we'll have them take one of just old friends.' Her voice implied that this was best, most intimate of all. 'Come here, Jebby, George – not you, Hamilton; this is just my friends – Sally –'

A little after that, what remained of formality disappeared and the hours flowed easily down the profuse stream of champagne. In the modern fashion, Hamilton Rutherford sat at the table with his arm about an old girl of his and assured his guests, which included not a few bewildered but enthusiastic Europeans, that the party was not nearly at an end; it was to reassemble at Zelli's after midnight. Michael saw Mrs Dandy, not quite over her illness, rise to go and become caught in polite group after group, and he spoke of it to one of her daughters, who thereupon forcibly abducted her mother and called her car. Michael felt very considerate and proud of himself after having done this, and drank much more champagne.

'It's amazing,' George Packman was telling him enthusiastically. 'This show will cost Ham about five thousand dollars, and I understand they'll be just about his last. But did he countermand a bottle of champagne or a flower? Not he! He happens to have it – that young man. Do you know that T. G. Vance offered him a salary of fifty thousand dollars a year ten minutes before the wedding this morning? In another year he'll be back with the millionaires.'

The conversation was interrupted by a plan to carry Rutherford out on communal shoulders – a plan which six of them put into effect, and then stood in the four-o'clock sunshine waving good-bye to the bride and groom. But there must have been a mistake somewhere, for five minutes later Michael saw both bride and groom descending the stairway to the reception, each with a glass of champagne held defiantly on high.

'This is our way of doing things,' he thought. 'Generous and fresh and free; a sort of Virginia-plantation hospitality, but at a different pace now, nervous as a ticker tape.'

Standing unselfconsciously in the middle of the room to see which was the American ambassador, he realized with a start that he hadn't really thought of Caroline for hours. He looked about him with a sort of alarm, and then he saw her across the room, very bright and young, and radiantly happy. He saw Rutherford near her, looking at her as if he could never look long enough, and as Michael watched them they seemed to recede as he had wished them to do that day in the Rue de Castiglione – recede and fade off into joys and griefs of their own, into the years that would take the toll of Rutherford's fine pride and Caroline's young, moving beauty; fade far away, so that now he could scarcely see them, as if they were shrouded in something as misty as her white, billowing dress.

Michael was cured. The ceremonial function, with its pomp and its revelry, had stood for a sort of initiation into a life where even his regret could not follow them. All the bitterness melted out of him suddenly and the world reconstituted itself out of the youth and happiness that was all around him, profligate as the spring sunshine. He was trying to remember which one of the bridesmaids he had made a date to dine with tonight as he walked forward to bid Hamilton and Caroline Rutherford good-bye.

Crazy Sunday

[1932]

I

It was Sunday – not a day, but rather a gap between two other days. Behind, for all of them, lay sets and sequences, the long waits under the crane that swung the microphone, the hundred miles a day by automobiles to and fro across a county, the struggles of rival ingenuities in the conference rooms, the ceaseless compromise, the clash and strain of many personalities fighting for their lives. And now Sunday, with individual life starting up again, with a glow kindling in eyes that had been glazed with monotony the afternoon before. Slowly as the hours waned they came awake like 'Puppenfeen' in a toy shop: an intense colloquy in a corner, lovers disappearing to neck in a hall. And the feeling of 'Hurry, it's not too late, but for God's sake hurry before the blessed forty hours of leisure are over.'

Joel Coles was writing continuity. He was twenty-eight and not yet broken by Hollywood. He had had what were considered nice assignments since his arrival six months before and he submitted his scenes and sequences with enthusiasm. He referred to himself modestly as a hack but really did not think of it that way. His mother had been a successful actress; Joel had spent his childhood between London and New York trying to separate the real from the unreal, or at least to keep one guess ahead. He was a handsome man with the pleasant cow-brown eyes that in 1913 had gazed out at Broadway audiences from his mother's face.

When the invitation came it made him sure that he was getting somewhere. Ordinarily he did not go out on Sundays but stayed sober and took work home with him. Recently they had given him a Eugene O'Neill play destined for a very important lady indeed. Everything he had done so far had pleased Miles

Calman, and Miles Calman was the only director on the lot who did not work under a supervisor and was responsible to the money men alone. Everything was clicking into place in Joel's career. ('This is Mr Calman's secretary. Will you come to tea from four to six Sunday – he lives in Beverly Hills, number –.')

Joel was flattered. It would be a party out of the top-drawer. It was a tribute to himself as a young man of promise. The Marion Davies crowd, the high-hats, the big currency numbers, perhaps even Dietrich and Garbo and the Marquis, people who were not seen everywhere, would probably be at Calman's.

'I won't take anything to drink,' he assured himself. Calman was audibly tired of rummies, and thought it was a pity the industry could not get along without them.

Joel agreed that writers drank too much – he did himself, but he wouldn't this afternoon. He wished Miles would be within hearing when the cocktails were passed to hear his succinct, unobtrusive, 'No, thank you.'

Miles Calman's house was built for great emotional moments – there was an air of listening, as if the far silences of its vistas hid an audience, but this afternoon it was thronged, as though people had been bidden rather than asked. Joel noted with pride that only two other writers from the studio were in the crowd, an ennobled limey and, somewhat to his surprise, Nat Keogh, who had evoked Calman's impatient comment on drunks.

Stella Calman (Stella Walker, of course) did not move on to her other guests after she spoke to Joel. She lingered – she looked at him with the sort of beautiful look that demands some sort of acknowledgment and Joel drew quickly on the dramatic adequacy inherited from his mother:

'Well, you look about sixteen! Where's your kiddy car?'

She was visibly pleased; she lingered. He felt that he should say something more, something confident and easy – he had first met her when she was struggling for bits in New York. At the moment a tray slid up and Stella put a cocktail glass into his hand.

'Everybody's afraid, aren't they?' he said, looking at it absently. 'Everybody watches for everybody else's blunders, or tries to make sure they're with people that'll do them credit. Of course that's not true in your house,' he covered himself hastily. 'I just meant generally in Hollywood.'

Stella agreed. She presented several people to Joel as if he were very important. Reassuring himself that Miles was at the other side of the room, Joel drank the cocktail.

'So you have a baby?' he said. 'That's the time to look out. After a pretty woman has had her first child, she's very vulnerable, because she wants to be reassured about her own charm. She's got to have some new man's unqualified devotion to prove to herself she hasn't lost anything.'

'I never get anybody's unqualified devotion,' Stella said rather resentfully.

'They're afraid of your husband.'

'You think that's it?' She wrinkled her brow over the idea; then the conversation was interrupted at the exact moment Joel would have chosen.

Her attentions had given him confidence. Not for him to join safe groups, to slink to refuge under the wings of such acquaintances as he saw about the room. He walked to the window and looked out towards the Pacific, colourless under its sluggish sunset. It was good here – the American Riviera and all that, if there were ever time to enjoy it. The handsome, well-dressed people in the room, the lovely girls, and the – well, the lovely girls. You couldn't have everything.

He saw Stella's fresh boyish face, with the tired eyelid that always drooped a little over one eye, moving about among her guests and he wanted to sit with her and talk a long time as if she were a girl instead of a name; he followed her to see if she paid anyone as much attention as she had paid him. He took another cocktail – not because he needed confidence but because she had given him so much of it. Then he sat down beside the director's mother.

'Your son's gotten to be a legend, Mrs Calman – Oracle and a Man of Destiny and all that. Personally, I'm against him but I'm in a minority. What do you think of him? Are you impressed? Are you surprised how far he's gone?'

'No, I'm not surprised,' she said calmly. 'We always expected a lot from Miles.'

'Well now, that's unusual,' remarked Joel. 'I always think all mothers are like Napoleon's mother. My mother didn't want me to have anything to do with the entertainment business. She wanted me to go to West Point and be safe.'

'We always had every confidence in Miles.' . . .

He stood by the built-in bar of the dining-room with the good-humoured, heavy-drinking, highly paid Nat Keogh.

'– I made a hundred grand during the year and lost forty grand gambling, so now I've hired a manager.'

'You mean an agent,' suggested Joel.

'No, I've got that too. I mean a manager. I make over everything to my wife and then he and my wife get together and hand me out the money. I pay him five thousand a year to hand me out my money.'

'You mean your agent.'

'No, I mean my manager, and I'm not the only one – a lot of other irresponsible people have him.'

'Well, if you're irresponsible why are you responsible enough to hire a manager?'

'I'm just irresponsible about gambling. Look here –'

A singer performed; Joel and Nat went forward with the others to listen.

2

The singing reached Joel vaguely; he felt happy and friendly towards all the people gathered there, people of bravery and industry, superior to bourgeoisie that outdid them in ignorance and loose living, risen to a position of the highest prominence in a nation that for a decade had wanted only to be entertained. He liked them – he loved them. Great waves of good feeling flowed through him.

As the singer finished his number and there was a drift towards the hostess to say good-bye, Joel had an idea. He would give them 'Building It Up', his own composition. It was his only parlour trick, it had amused several parties and it might please Stella Walker. Possessed by the hunch, his blood throbbing with the scarlet corpuscles of exhibitionism, he sought her.

'Of course,' she cried. 'Please ! Do you need anything?'

'Someone has to be the secretary that I'm supposed to be dictating to.'

'I'll be her.'

As the word spread, the guests in the hall, already putting on their coats to leave, drifted back and Joel faced the eyes of many strangers. He had a dim foreboding, realizing that the man who had just performed was a famous radio entertainer. Then someone said 'Sh!' and he was alone with Stella, the centre of a sinister Indian-like half-circle. Stella smiled up at him expectantly – he began.

His burlesque was based upon the cultural limitations of Mr Dave Silverstein, an independent producer; Silverstein was presumed to be dictating a letter outlining a treatment of a story he had bought.

'– a story of divorce, the young generators and the Foreign Legion,' he heard his voice saying, with the intonations of Mr Silverstein. 'But we got to build it up, see?'

A sharp pang of doubt struck through him. The faces surrounding him in the gently moulded light were intent and curious, but there was no ghost of a smile anywhere; directly in front the Great Lover of the screen glared at him with an eye as keen as the eye of a potato. Only Stella Walker looked up at him with a radiant, never faltering smile.

'If we make him a Menjou type, then we get a sort of Michael Arlen only with a Honolulu atmosphere.'

Still not a ripple in front, but in the rear a rustling, a perceptible shift towards the left, towards the front door.

'– then she says she feels this sex appil for him and he burns out and says, "Oh, go on destroy yourself –"'

At some point he heard Nat Keogh snicker and here and there were a few encouraging faces, but as he finished he had the sickening realization that he had made a fool of himself in view

99

of an important section of the picture world, upon whose favour depended his career.

For a moment he existed in the midst of a confused silence, broken by a general trek for the door. He felt the undercurrent of derision that rolled through the gossip; then – all this was in the space of ten seconds – the Great Lover, his eye hard and empty as the eye of a needle, shouted 'Boo! Boo!' voicing in an overtone what he felt was the mood of the crowd. It was the resentment of the professional towards the amateur, of the community towards the stranger, the thumbs-down of the clan.

Only Stella Walker was still standing near and thanking him as if he had been an unparalleled success, as if it hadn't occurred to her that anyone hadn't liked it. As Nat Keogh helped him into his overcoat, a great wave of self-disgust swept over him and he clung desperately to his rule of never betraying an inferior emotion until he no longer felt it.

'I was a flop,' he said lightly, to Stella. 'Never mind, it's a good number when appreciated. Thanks for your cooperation.'

The smile did not leave her face – he bowed rather drunkenly and Nat drew him towards the door. . . .

The arrival of his breakfast awakened him into a broken and ruined world. Yesterday he was himself, a point of fire against an industry, today he felt that he was pitted under an enormous disadvantage, against those faces, against individual contempt and collective sneer. Worse than that, to Miles Calman he was become one of those rummies, stripped of dignity, whom Calman regretted he was compelled to use. To Stella Walker on whom he had forced a martyrdom to preserve the courtesy of her house – her opinion he did not dare to guess. His gastric juices ceased to flow and he set his poached eggs back on the telephone table. He wrote:

Dear Miles: You can imagine my profound self-disgust. I confess to a taint of exhibitionism, but at six o'clock in the afternoon, in broad daylight! Good God! My apologies to your wife.

Yours ever,
Joel Coles.

Joel emerged from his office on the lot only to slink like a malefactor to the tobacco store. So suspicious was his manner that one of the studio police asked to see his admission card. He had decided to eat lunch outside when Nat Keogh, confident and cheerful, overtook him.

'What do you mean you're in permanent retirement? What if that Three-Piece Suit did boo you?

'Why listen,' he continued, drawing Joel into the studio restaurant. 'The night of one of his premières at Grauman's, Joe Squires kicked his tail while he was bowing to the crowd. The ham said Joe'd hear from him later but when Joe called him up at eight o'clock next day and said, "I thought I was going to hear from you," he hung up the phone.'

The preposterous story cheered Joel, and he found a gloomy consolation in staring at the group at the next table, the sad, lovely Siamese twins, the mean dwarfs, the proud giant from the circus picture. But looking beyond at the yellow-stained faces of pretty women, their eyes all melancholy and startling with mascara, their ball gowns garish in full day, he saw a group who had been at Calman's and winced.

'Never again,' he exclaimed aloud, 'absolutely my last social appearance in Hollywood!'

The following morning a telegram was waiting for him at his office:

You were one of the most agreeable people at our party. Expect you at my sister June's buffet supper next Sunday.

Stella Walker Calman.

The blood rushed fast through his veins for a feverish minute. Incredulously he read the telegram over.

'Well, that's the sweetest thing I ever heard of in my life!'

3

Crazy Sunday again. Joel slept until eleven, then he read a newspaper to catch up with the past week. He lunched in his room on trout, avocado salad and a pint of California wine. Dressing for the tea, he selected a pin-check suit, a blue shirt, a burnt orange tie. There were dark circles of fatigue under his eyes. In his second-hand car he drove to the Riviera apartments. As he was introducing himself to Stella's sister, Miles and Stella arrived in riding clothes – they had been quarrelling fiercely most of the afternoon on all the dirt roads back of Beverly Hills.

Miles Calman, tall, nervous, with a desperate humour and the unhappiest eyes Joel ever saw, was an artist from the top of his curiously shaped head to his niggerish feet. Upon these last he stood firmly – he had never made a cheap picture though he had sometimes paid heavily for the luxury of making experimental flops. In spite of his excellent company, one could not be with him long without realizing that he was not a well man.

From the moment of their entrance Joel's day bound itself up inextricably with theirs. As he joined the group around them Stella turned away from it with an impatient little tongue click – and Miles Calman said to the man who happened to be next to him:

'Go easy on Eva Goebel. There's hell to pay about her at home.' Miles turned to Joel, 'I'm sorry I missed you at the office yesterday. I spent the afternoon at the analyst's.'

'You being psychoanalysed?'

'I have been for months. First I went for claustrophobia, now I'm trying to get my whole life cleared up. They say it'll take over a year.'

'There's nothing the matter with your life,' Joel assured him.

'Oh, no? Well, Stella seems to think so. Ask anybody – they can all tell you about it,' he said bitterly.

A girl perched herself on the arm of Miles's chair; Joel crossed to Stella, who stood disconsolately by the fire.

'Thank you for your telegram,' he said. 'It was darn sweet. I can't imagine anybody as good-looking as you are being so good-humoured.'

She was a little lovelier than he had ever seen her and perhaps the unstinted admiration in his eyes prompted her to unload on him – it did not take long, for she was obviously at the emotional bursting point.

'– and Miles has been carrying on this thing for two years, and I never knew. Why, she was one of my best friends, always in the house. Finally when people began to come to me, Miles had to admit it.'

She sat down vehemently on the arm of Joel's chair. Her riding breeches were the colour of the chair and Joel saw that the mass of her hair was made up of some strands of red gold and some of pale gold, so that it could not be dyed, and that she had on no make-up. She was that good-looking –

Still quivering with the shock of her discovery, Stella found unbearable the spectacle of a new girl hovering over Miles; she led Joel into a bedroom, and seated at either end of a big bed they went on talking. People on their way to the washroom glanced in and made wisecracks, but Stella, emptying out her story, paid no attention. After a while Miles stuck his head in the door and said, 'There's no use trying to explain something to Joel in half an hour that I don't understand myself and the psychoanalyst says will take a whole year to understand.'

She talked on as if Miles were not there. She loved Miles, she said – under considerable difficulties she had always been faithful to him.

'The psychoanalyst told Miles that he had a mother complex. In his first marriage he transferred his mother complex to his wife, you see – and then his sex turned to me. But when we married the thing repeated itself – he transferred his mother complex to me and all his libido turned towards this other woman.'

Joel knew that this probably wasn't gibberish – yet it sounded like gibberish. He knew Eva Goebel; she was a motherly person, older and probably wiser than Stella, who was a golden child.

Miles now suggested impatiently that Joel come back with them since Stella had so much to say, so they drove out to the mansion in Beverly Hills. Under the high ceilings the situation seemed more dignified and tragic. It was an eerie bright night with the dark very clear outside of all the windows and Stella all rose-gold raging and crying around the room. Joel did not quite believe in picture actresses' grief. They have other pre-occupations – they are beautiful rose-gold figures blown full of life by writers and directors, and after hours they sit around and talk in whispers and giggle innuendoes, and the ends of many adventures flow through them.

Sometimes he pretended to listen and instead thought how well she was got up – sleek breeches with a matched set of legs in them, an Italian-coloured sweater with a little high neck, and a short brown chamois coat. He couldn't decide whether she was an imitation of an English lady or an English lady was an imitation of her. She hovered somewhere between the realest of realities and the most blatant of impersonations.

'Miles is so jealous of me that he questions everything I do,' she cried scornfully. 'When I was in New York I wrote him that I'd been to the theatre with Eddie Baker. Miles was so jealous he phoned me ten times in one day.'

'I was wild,' Miles snuffled sharply, a habit he had in times of stress. 'The analyst couldn't get any results for a week.'

Stella shook her head despairingly. 'Did you expect me just to sit in the hotel for three weeks?'

'I don't expect anything. I admit that I'm jealous. I try not to be. I worked on that with Dr Bridgebane, but it didn't do any good. I was jealous of Joel this afternoon when you sat on the arm of his chair.'

'You were?' She started up. 'You were! Wasn't there some-body on the arm of your chair? And did you speak to me for two hours?'

'You were telling your troubles to Joel in the bedroom.'

'When I think that that woman' – she seemed to believe that to omit Eva Goebel's name would be to lessen her reality – 'used to come here –'

'All right – all right,' said Miles wearily. 'I've admitted every-thing and I feel as bad about it as you do.' Turning to Joel he began talking about pictures, while Stella moved restlessly along the far walls, her hands in her breeches pockets.

'They've treated Miles terribly,' she said, coming suddenly back into the conversation as if they'd never discussed her personal affairs. 'Dear, tell him about old Beltzer trying to change your picture.'

As she stood hovering protectively over Miles, her eyes flashing with indignation in his behalf, Joel realized that he was in love with her. Stifled with excitement he got up to say good night.

With Monday the week resumed its workaday rhythm, in sharp contrast to the theoretical discussions, the gossip and scandal of Sunday; there was the endless detail of script revision – 'Instead of a lousy dissolve, we can leave her voice on the sound track and cut to a medium shot of the taxi from Bell's angle or we can simply pull the camera back to include the station, hold it a minute and then pan to the row of taxis' – by Monday afternoon Joel had again forgotten that people whose business was to provide entertainment were ever privileged to be entertained. In the evening he phoned Miles's house. He asked for Miles but Stella came to the phone.

'Do things seem better?'

'Not particularly. What are you doing next Saturday evening?'

'Nothing.'

'The Perrys are giving a dinner and theatre party and Miles won't be here – he's flying to South Bend to see the Notre Dame-California game. I thought you might go with me in his place.'

After a long moment Joel said, 'Why – surely. If there's a conference I can't make dinner but I can get to the theatre.'

'Then I'll say we can come.'

Joel walked to his office. In view of the strained relations of the Calmans, would Miles be pleased, or did she intend that Miles shouldn't know of it? That would be out of the question – if Miles didn't mention it Joel would. But it was an hour or more before he could get down to work again.

Wednesday there was a four-hour wrangle in a conference room crowded with planets and nebulae of cigarette smoke. Three men and a woman paced the carpet in turn, suggesting or condemning, speaking sharply or persuasively, confidently or despairingly. At the end Joel lingered to talk to Miles.

The man was tired – not with the exaltation of fatigue but life-tired, with his lids sagging and his beard prominent over the blue shadows near his mouth.

'I hear you're flying to the Notre Dame game.'

Miles looked beyond him and shook his head.

'I've given up the idea.'

'Why?'

'On account of you.' Still he did not look at Joel.

'What the hell, Miles?'

'That's why I've given it up.' He broke into a perfunctory laugh at himself. 'I can't tell what Stella might do just out of spite – she's invited you to take her to the Perrys', hasn't she? I wouldn't enjoy the game.'

The fine instinct that moved swiftly and confidently on the set muddled so weakly and helplessly through his personal life.

'Look, Miles,' Joel said frowning. 'I've never made any passes whatsoever at Stella. If you're really seriously cancelling your trip on account of me, I won't go to the Perrys' with her. I won't see her. You can trust me absolutely.'

Miles looked at him, carefully now.

'Maybe.' He shrugged his shoulders. 'Anyhow there'd just be somebody else. I wouldn't have any fun.'

'You don't seem to have much confidence in Stella. She told me she'd always been true to you.'

'Maybe she has.' In the last few minutes several more muscles had sagged around Miles's mouth. 'But how can I ask anything of her after what's happened? How can I expect her –' He broke off and his face grew harder as he said, 'I'll tell you one thing, right or wrong and no matter what I've done, if I ever had anything on her I'd divorce her. I can't have my pride hurt – that would be the last straw.'

His tone annoyed Joel, but he said:

'Hasn't she calmed down about the Eva Goebel thing?'

'No.' Miles snuffled pessimistically. 'I can't get over it either.'

'I thought it was finished.'

'I'm trying not to see Eva again, but you know it isn't easy just to drop something like that – it isn't some girl I kissed last night in a taxi. The psychoanalyst says –'

'I know,' Joel interrupted. 'Stella told me.' This was depressing. 'Well, as far as I'm concerned if you go to the game I won't see Stella. And I'm sure Stella has nothing on her conscience about anybody.'

'Maybe not,' Miles repeated listlessly. 'Anyhow I'll stay and take her to the party. Say,' he said suddenly, 'I wish you'd come too. I've got to have somebody sympathetic to talk to. That's the trouble – I've influenced Stella in everything. Especially I've influenced her so that she likes all the men I like – it's very difficult.'

'It must be,' Joel agreed.

4

Joel could not get to the dinner. Self-conscious in his silk hat against the unemployment, he waited for the others in front of the Hollywood Theatre and watched the evening parade: obscure replicas of bright, particular picture stars, spavined men in polo coats, a stomping dervish with the beard and staff of an apostle, a pair of chic Filipinos in collegiate clothes, reminder that this corner of the Republic opened to the seven seas, a long fantastic carnival of young shouts which proved to be a fraternity initiation. The line split to pass two smart limousines that stopped at the kerb.

There she was, in a dress like ice-water, made in a thousand pale-blue pieces, with icicles trickling at the throat. He started forward.

'So you like my dress?'

'Where's Miles?'

'He flew to the game after all. He left yesterday morning – at least I think –' She broke off. 'I just got a telegram from South Bend saying that he's starting back. I forgot – you know all these people?'

The party of eight moved into the theatre.

Miles had gone after all and Joel wondered if he should have come. But during the performance, with Stella a profile under the pure grain of light hair, he thought no more about Miles. Once he turned and looked at her and she looked back at him, smiling and meeting his eyes for as long as he wanted. Between the acts they smoked in the lobby and she whispered:

'They're all going to the opening of Jack Johnson's night club – I don't want to go, do you?'

'Do we have to?'

'I suppose not.' She hesitated. 'I'd like to talk to you. I suppose we could go to our house – if I were only sure –'

Again she hesitated and Joel asked:

'Sure of what?'

'Sure that – oh, I'm haywire I know, but how can I be sure Miles went to the game?'

'You mean you think he's with Eva Goebel?'

'No, not so much that – but supposing he was here watching everything I do. You know Miles does odd things sometimes. Once he wanted a man with a long beard to drink tea with him and he sent down to the casting agency for one, and drank tea with him all afternoon.'

'That's different. He sent you a wire from South Bend – that proves he's at the game.'

After the play they said good night to the others at the kerb and were answered by looks of amusement. They slid off along the golden garish thoroughfare through the crowd that had gathered around Stella.

'You see he could arrange the telegrams,' Stella said, 'very easily.'

That was true. And with the idea that perhaps her uneasiness was justified, Joel grew angry: if Miles had trained a camera on them he felt no obligations towards Miles. Aloud he said:

'That's nonsense.'

There were Christmas trees already in the shop windows and the full moon over the boulevard was only a prop, as scenic as the giant boudoir lamps of the corners. On into the dark foliage of Beverly Hills that flamed as eucalyptus by day, Joel saw only

the flash of a white face under his own, the arc of her shoulder.
She pulled away suddenly and looked up at him.

'Your eyes are like your mother's,' she said. 'I used to have a
scrap book full of pictures of her.'

'Your eyes are like your own and not a bit like any other
eyes,' he answered.

Something made Joel look out into the grounds as they went
into the house, as if Miles were lurking in the shubbery. A telegram waited on the hall table. She read aloud:

> Chicago.
>
> 'Home tomorrow night. Thinking of you. Love.
>
> Miles.'

'You see,' she said, throwing the slip back on the table, 'he
could easily have faked that.' She asked the butler for drinks
and sandwiches and ran upstairs, while Joel walked into the
empty reception rooms. Strolling about he wandered to the
piano where he had stood in disgrace two Sundays before.

'Then we could put over,' he said aloud, 'a story of divorce,
the younger generation and the Foreign Legion.'

His thoughts jumped to another telegram.

'You were one of the most agreeable people at our party—'

An idea occurred to him. If Stella's telegram had been purely
a gesture of courtesy then it was likely that Miles had inspired
it, for it was Miles who had invited him. Probably Miles had
said:

'Send him a wire – he's miserable – he thinks he's queered
himself.'

It fitted in with 'I've influenced Stella in everything. Especially I've influenced her so that she likes all the men I like.' A
woman would do a thing like that because she felt sympathetic
– only a man would do it because he felt responsible.

When Stella came back into the room he took both her hands.

'I have a strange feeling that I'm a sort of pawn in a spite
game you're playing against Miles,' he said.

'Help yourself to a drink.'

'And the odd thing is that I'm in love with you anyhow.'

The telephone rang and she freed herself to answer it.

'Another wire from Miles,' she announced. 'He dropped it, or it says he dropped it, from the aeroplane at Kansas City.'

'I suppose he asked to be remembered to me.'

'No, he just said he loved me. I believe he does. He's so very weak.'

'Come sit beside me,' Joel urged her.

It was early. And it was still a few minutes short of midnight a half-hour later, when Joel walked to the cold hearth, and said tersely:

'Meaning that you haven't any curiosity about me?'

'Not at all. You attract me a lot and you know it. The point is that I suppose I really do love Miles.'

'Obviously.'

'And tonight I feel uneasy about everything.'

He wasn't angry – he was even faintly relieved that a possible entanglement was avoided. Still as he looked at her, the warmth and softness of her body thawing her cold blue costume, he knew she was one of the things he would always regret.

'I've got to go,' he said. 'I'll phone a taxi.'

'Nonsense – there's a chauffeur on duty.'

He winced at her readiness to have him go, and seeing this she kissed him lightly and said, 'You're sweet, Joel.' Then suddenly three things happened: he took down his drink at a gulp, the phone rang loud through the house and a clock in the hall struck in trumpet notes.

Nine – ten – eleven – twelve –

5

It was Sunday again. Joel realized that he had come to the theatre this evening with the work of the week still hanging about him like cerements. He had made love to Stella as he might attack some matter to be cleaned up hurriedly before the day's end. But this was Sunday – the lovely, lazy perspective of the next twenty-four hours unrolled before him – every minute was something to be approached with lulling indirection, every moment held the germ of innumerable possibilities. Nothing was impossible – everything was just beginning. He poured himself another drink.

With a sharp moan, Stella slipped forward inertly by the telephone. Joel picked her up and laid her on the sofa. He squirted soda-water on a handkerchief and slapped it over her face. The telephone mouthpiece was still grinding and he put it to his ear.

'– the plane fell just this side of Kansas City. The body of Miles Calman has been identified and –'

He hung up the receiver.

'Lie still,' he said, stalling, as Stella opened her eyes.

'Oh, what's happened?' she whispered. 'Call them back. Oh, what's happened?'

'I'll call them right away. What's your doctor's name?'

'Did they say Miles was dead?'

'Lie quiet – is there a servant still up?'

'Hold me – I'm frightened.'

He put his arm around her.

'I want the name of your doctor,' he said sternly. 'It may be a mistake but I want someone here.'

'It's Doctor – Oh, God, is Miles dead?'

Joel ran upstairs and searched through strange medicine cabinets for spirits of ammonia. When he came down Stella cried:

'He isn't dead – I know he isn't. This is part of his scheme. He's torturing me. I know he's alive. I can feel he's alive.'

'I want to get hold of some close friend of yours, Stella. You can't stay here alone tonight.'

'Oh, no,' she cried. 'I can't see anybody. You stay, I haven't got any friend.' She got up, tears streaming down her face. 'Oh, Miles is my only friend. He's not dead – he can't be dead. I'm going there right away and see. Get a train. You'll have to come with me.'

'You can't. There's nothing to do tonight. I want you to tell me the name of some woman I can call: Lois? Joan? Carmel? Isn't there somebody?'

Stella stared at him blindly.

'Eva Goebel was my best friend,' she said.

Joel thought of Miles, his sad and desperate face in the office two days before. In the awful silence of his death all was clear about him. He was the only American-born director with both an interesting temperament and an artistic conscience. Meshed in an industry, he had paid with his ruined nerves for having no resilience, no healthy cynicism, no refuge – only a pitiful and precarious escape.

There was a sound at the outer door – it opened suddenly, and there were footsteps in the hall.

'Miles!' Stella screamed. 'Is it you, Miles? Oh, it's Miles.'

A telegraph boy appeared in the doorway.

'I couldn't find the bell. I heard you talking inside.'

The telegram was a duplicate of the one that had been phoned. While Stella read it over and over, as though it were a black lie, Joel telephoned. It was still early and he had difficulty getting anyone; when finally he succeeded in finding some friends he made Stella take a stiff drink.

'You'll stay here, Joel,' she whispered, as though she were half-asleep. 'You won't go away. Miles liked you – he said you –' She shivered violently, 'Oh, my God, you don't know how alone I feel!' Her eyes closed, 'Put your arms around me. Miles had a suit like that.' She started bolt upright. 'Think of what he must have felt. He was afraid of almost everything, anyhow.'

She shook her head dazedly. Suddenly she seized Joel's face and held it close to hers.

'You won't go. You like me – you love me, don't you? Don't call up anybody. Tomorrow's time enough. You stay here with me tonight.'

He stared at her, at first incredulously, and then with shocked understanding. In her dark groping Stella was trying to keep Miles alive by sustaining a situation in which he had figured – as if Miles's mind could not die so long as the possibilities that had worried him still existed. It was a distraught and tortured effort to stave off the realization that he was dead.

Resolutely Joel went to the phone and called a doctor.

'Don't, oh, don't call anybody!' Stella cried. 'Come back here and put your arms around me.'

'Is Doctor Bales in?'

'Joel,' Stella cried. 'I thought I could count on you. Miles liked you. He was jealous of you – Joel, come here.'

Ah then – if he betrayed Miles she would be keeping him alive – for if he were really dead how could he be betrayed?

'– has just had a very severe shock. Can you come at once, and get hold of a nurse?'

'Joel!'

Now the door-bell and the telephone began to ring intermittently, and automobiles were stopping in front of the door.

'But you're not going,' Stella begged him. 'You're going to stay, aren't you?'

'No,' he answered. 'But I'll be back, if you need me.'

Standing on the steps of the house which now hummed and palpitated with the life that flutters around death like protective leaves, he began to sob a little in his throat.

'Everything he touched he did something magical to,' he thought. 'He even brought that little gamine alive and made her a sort of masterpiece.'

And then:

'What a hell of a hole he leaves in this damn wilderness – already!'

And then with a certain bitterness, 'Oh, yes, I'll be back – I'll be back!'

Three Hours between Planes

[1941]

I

It was a wild chance but Donald was in the mood, healthy and bored, with a sense of tiresome duty done. He was now rewarding himself. Maybe.

When the plane landed he stepped out into a mid-western summer night and headed for the isolated pueblo airport, conventionalized as an old red 'railway depot'. He did not know whether she was alive, or living in this town, or what was her present name. With mounting excitement he looked through the phone book for her father who might be dead too, somewhere in these twenty years.

No. Judge Harmon Holmes – Hillside 3194.

A woman's amused voice answered his inquiry for Miss Nancy Holmes.

'Nancy is Mrs Walter Gifford now. Who is this?'

But Donald hung up without answering. He had found out what he wanted to know and had only three hours. He did not remember any Walter Gifford and there was another suspended moment while he scanned the phone book. She might have married out of town.

No. Walter Gifford – Hillside 1191. Blood flowed back into his fingertips.

'Hello?'

'Hello. Is Mrs Gifford there – this is an old friend of hers.'

'This is Mrs Gifford.'

He remembered, or thought he remembered, the funny magic in the voice.

'This is Donald Plant. I haven't seen you since I was twelve years old.'

'Oh-h-h!' The note was utterly surprised, very polite, but

he could distinguish in it neither joy nor certain recognition.

'– *Donald*!' added the voice. This time there was something more in it than struggling memory.

'... when did you come back to town?' Then cordially, 'Where *are* you?'

'I'm out at the airport – for just a few hours.'

'Well, come up and see me.'

'Sure you're not just going to bed.'

'Heavens, no!' she exclaimed. 'I was sitting here – having a highball by myself. Just tell your taxi man ...'

On his way Donald analysed the conversation. His words 'at the airport' established that he had retained his position in the upper bourgeoisie. Nancy's aloneness might indicate that she had matured into an unattractive woman without friends. Her husband might be either away or in bed. And – because she was always ten years old in his dreams – the highball shocked him. But he adjusted himself with a smile – she was very close to thirty.

At the end of a curved drive he saw a dark-haired little beauty standing against the lighted door, a glass in her hand. Startled by her final materialization, Donald got out of the cab, saying:

'Mrs Gifford?'

She turned on the porch light and stared at him, wide-eyed and tentative. A smile broke through the puzzled expression.

'Donald – it is you – we all change so. Oh, this is remarkable!'

As they walked inside, their voices jingled the words 'all these years', and Donald felt a sinking in his stomach. This derived in part from a vision of their last meeting – when she rode past him on a bicycle, cutting him dead – and in part from fear lest they have nothing to say. It was like a college reunion – but there the failure to find the past was disguised by the hurried boisterous occasion. Aghast, he realized that this might be a long and empty hour. He plunged in desperately.

'You always were a lovely person. But I'm a little shocked to find you as beautiful as you are.'

It worked. The immediate recognition of their changed state, the bold compliment, made them interesting strangers instead of fumbling childhood friends.

'Have a highball?' she asked. 'No? Please don't think I've become a secret drinker, but this was a blue night. I expected my husband but he wired he'd be two days longer. He's very nice, Donald, and very attractive. Rather your type and colouring.' She hesitated, '– and I think he's interested in someone in New York – and I don't know.'

'After seeing you it sounds impossible,' he assured her. 'I was married for six years, and there was a time I tortured myself that way. Then one day I just put jealousy out of my life forever. After my wife died I was very glad of that. It left a very rich memory – nothing marred or spoiled or hard to think over.'

She looked at him attentively, then sympathetically as he spoke.

'I'm very sorry,' she said. And after a proper moment, 'You've changed a lot. Turn your head. I remember father saying, "That boy has a brain".'

'You probably argued against it.'

'I was impressed. Up to then I thought everybody had a brain. That's why it sticks in my mind.'

'What else sticks in your mind?' he asked smiling.

Suddenly Nancy got up and walked quickly a little away.

'Ah, now,' she reproached him. 'That isn't fair! I suppose I was a naughty girl.'

'You were not,' he said stoutly. 'And I *will* have a drink now.'

As she poured it, her face still turned from him, he continued:

'Do you think you were the only little girl who was ever kissed?'

'Do you like the subject?' she demanded. Her momentary irritation melted and she said: 'What the hell! We *did* have fun. Like in the song.'

'On the sleigh ride.'

'Yes – and somebody's picnic – Trudy James's. And at Frontenac that – those summers.'

It was the sleigh ride he remembered most and kissing her cool cheeks in the straw in one corner while she laughed up at the cold white stars. The couple next to them had their backs turned and he kissed her little neck and her ears and never her lips.

'And the Macks' party where they played post office and I couldn't go because I had the mumps,' he said.

'I don't remember that.'

'Oh, you were there. And you were kissed and I was crazy with jealousy like I never have been since.'

'Funny I don't remember. Maybe I wanted to forget.'

'But why?' he asked in amusement. 'We were two perfectly innocent kids. Nancy, whenever I talked to my wife about the past, I told her you were the girl I loved *al*most as much as I loved her. But I think I really loved you just as much. When we moved out of town I carried you like a cannon ball in my insides.'

'Were you *that* much – stirred up?'

'My God, yes! I –' He suddenly realized that they were standing just two feet from each other, that he was talking as if he loved her in the present, that she was looking up at him with her lips half-parted and a clouded look in her eyes.

'Go on,' she said, 'I'm ashamed to say – I like it. I didn't know you were so upset *then*. I thought it was *me* who was upset.'

'You!' he exclaimed. 'Don't you remember throwing me over at the drugstore.' He laughed. 'You stuck out your tongue at me.'

'I don't remember at all. It seemed to me *you* did the throwing over.' Her hand fell lightly, almost consolingly on his arm. 'I've got a photograph book upstairs I haven't looked at for years. I'll dig it out.'

Donald sat for five minutes with two thoughts – first the hopeless impossibility of reconciling what different people remembered about the same event – and secondly that in a frightening way Nancy moved him as a woman as she had moved him as a child. Half an hour had developed an emotion that he had not known since the death of his wife – that he had never hoped to know again.

Side by side on a couch they opened the book between them. Nancy looked at him, smiling and very happy.

'Oh, this is *such* fun,' she said. 'Such fun that you're so nice, that you remember me so – beautifully. Let me tell you – I wish I'd known it then! After you'd gone I hated you.'

'What a pity,' he said gently.

'But not now,' she reassured him, and then impulsively, 'Kiss and make up –

'... that isn't being a good wife,' she said after a minute. 'I really don't think I've kissed two men since I was married.'

He was excited – but most of all confused. Had he kissed Nancy? or a memory? or this lovely trembly stranger who looked away from him quickly and turned a page of the book?

'Wait!' he said. 'I don't think I could *see* a picture for a few seconds.'

'We won't do it again. I don't feel so very calm myself.'

Donald said one of those trivial things that cover so much ground.

'Wouldn't it be awful if we fell in love again?'

'Stop it!' She laughed, but very breathlessly. 'It's all over. It was a moment. A moment I'll have to forget.'

'Don't tell your husband.'

'Why not? Usually I tell him everything.'

'It'll hurt him. Don't ever tell a man such things.'

'All right I won't.'

'Kiss me once more,' he said inconsistently, but Nancy had turned a page and was pointing eagerly at a picture.

'Here's you,' she cried. 'Right away!'

He looked. It was a little boy in shorts standing on a pier with a sailboat in the background.

'I remember –' she laughed triumphantly, '– the very day it was taken. Kitty took it and I stole it from her.'

For a moment Donald failed to recognize himself in the photo – then, bending closer – he failed utterly to recognize himself.

'That's not me,' he said.

'Oh yes. It was at Frontenac – the summer we – we used to go to the cave.'

'What cave? I was only three days in Frontenac.' Again he strained his eyes at the slightly yellowed picture. 'And that isn't me. That's Donald *Bowers*. We did look rather alike.'

Now she was staring at him – leaning back, seeming to lift away from him.

'But you're Donald Bowers!' she exclaimed; her voice rose a little. 'No, you're not. You're Donald *Plant*.'

'I told you on the phone.'

She was on her feet – her face faintly horrified.

'Plant! Bowers! I must be crazy. Or it was that drink? I was mixed up a little when I first saw you. Look here! What have I told you?'

He tried for a monkish calm as he turned a page of the book.

'Nothing at all,' he said. Pictures that did not include him formed and re-formed before his eyes – Frontenac – a cave – Donald Bowers – 'You threw *me* over!'

Nancy spoke from the other side of the room.

'You'll never tell this story,' she said. 'Stories have a way of getting around.'

'There isn't any story,' he hesitated. But he thought: So she was a bad little girl.

And now suddenly he was filled with wild raging jealousy of little Donald Bowers – he who had banished jealousy from his life forever. In the five steps he took across the room he crushed out twenty years and the existence of Walter Gifford with his stride.

'Kiss me again, Nancy,' he said, sinking to one knee beside her chair, putting his hand upon her shoulder. But Nancy strained away.

'You said you had to catch a plane.'

'It's nothing. I can miss it. It's of no importance.'

'Please go,' she said in a cool voice. 'And please try to imagine how I feel.'

'But you act as if you don't remember me,' he cried, '– as if you don't remember Donald *Plant*!'

'I do. I remember you too ... But it was all so long ago.' Her voice grew hard again. 'The taxi number is Crestwood 8484.'

On his way to the airport Donald shook his head from side to side. He was completely himself now but he could not digest the experience. Only as the plane roared up into the dark sky and its passengers became a different entity from the corporate world below did he draw a parallel from the fact of its flight. For five blinding minutes he had lived like a madman in two worlds at once. He had been a boy of twelve and a man of thirty-two, indissolubly and helplessly commingled.

Donald had lost a good deal, too, in those hours between the planes – but since the second half of life is a long process of getting rid of things, that part of the experience probably didn't matter.

The Lost Decade

[1939]

I

All sorts of people came into the offices of the newsweekly and Orrison Brown had all sorts of relations with them. Outside of office hours he was 'one of the editors' – during work time he was simply a curly-haired man who a year before had edited the Dartmouth *Jack-O-Lantern* and was now only too glad to take the undesirable assignments around the office, from straightening out illegible copy to playing call boy without the title.

He had seen this visitor go into the editor's office – a pale, tall man of forty with blond statuesque hair and a manner that was neither shy nor timid, nor otherworldly like a monk, but something of all three. The name on his card, Louis Trimble, evoked some vague memory, but having nothing to start on, Orrison did not puzzle over it – until a buzzer sounded on his desk, and previous experience warned him that Mr Trimble was to be his first course at lunch.

'Mr Trimble – Mr Brown,' said the Source of all luncheon money. 'Orrison – Mr Trimble's been away a long time. Or he *feels* it's a long time – almost twelve years. Some people would consider themselves lucky to've missed the last decade.'

'That's so,' said Orrison.

'I can't lunch today,' continued his chief. 'Take him to Voisin or 21 or anywhere he'd like. Mr Trimble feels there're lots of things he hasn't seen.'

Trimble demurred politely.

'Oh, I can get around.'

'I know it, old boy. Nobody knew this place like you did once – and if Brown tries to explain the horseless carriage just send him back here to me. And you'll be back yourself by four, won't you?'

Orrison got his hat.

'You've been away ten years?' he asked while they went down in the elevator.

'They'd begun the Empire State Building,' said Trimble. 'What does that add up to?'

'About 1928. But as the chief said, you've been lucky to miss a lot.' As a feeler he added, 'Probably had more interesting things to look at.'

'Can't say I have.'

They reached the street and the way Trimble's face tightened at the roar of traffic made Orrison take one more guess.

'You've been out of civilization?'

'In a sense.' The words were spoken in such a measured way that Orrison concluded this man wouldn't talk unless he wanted to – and simultaneously wondered if he could have possibly spent the thirties in a prison or an insane asylum.

'This is the famous 21,' he said. 'Do you think you'd rather eat somewhere else?'

Trimble paused, looking carefully at the brownstone house.

'I can remember when the name 21 got to be famous,' he said, 'about the same year as Moriarity's.' Then he continued almost apologetically, 'I thought we might walk up Fifth Avenue about five minutes and eat wherever we happened to be. Some place with young people to look at.'

Orrison gave him a quick glance and once again thought of bars and grey walls and bars; he wondered if his duties included introducing Mr Trimble to complaisant girls. But Mr Trimble didn't look as if that was in his mind – the dominant expression was of absolute and deep-seated curiosity and Orrison attempted to connect the name with Admiral Byrd's hideout at the South Pole or flyers lost in Brazilian jungles. He was, or he had been, quite a fellow – that was obvious. But the only definite clue to his environment – and to Orrison the clue that led nowhere – was his countryman's obedience to the traffic lights and his predilection for walking on the side next to the shops and not the street. Once he stopped and gazed into a haberdasher's window.

'Crêpe ties,' he said. 'I haven't seen one since I left college.'

'Where'd you go?'

'Massachusetts Tech.'

'Great place.'

'I'm going to take a look at it next week. Let's eat somewhere along here –' They were in the upper Fifties '– you choose.'

There was a good restaurant with a little awning just around the corner.

'What do you want to see most?' Orrison asked, as they sat down.

Trimble considered.

'Well – the back of people's heads,' he suggested. 'Their necks – how their heads are joined to their bodies. I'd like to hear what those two little girls are saying to their father. Not exactly what they're saying but whether the words float or submerge, how their mouths shut when they've finished speaking. Just a matter of rhythm – Cole Porter came back to the States in 1928 because he felt that there were new rhythms around.'

Orrison was sure he had his clue now, and with nice delicacy did not pursue it by a millimetre – even suppressing a sudden desire to say there was a fine concert in Carnegie Hall to-night.

'The weight of spoons,' said Trimble, 'so light. A little bowl with a stick attached. The cast in that waiter's eye. I knew him once but he wouldn't remember me.'

But as they left the restaurant the same waiter looked at Trimble rather puzzled as if he almost knew him. When they were outside Orrison laughed:

'After ten years people will forget.'

'Oh, I had dinner there last May –' He broke off in an abrupt manner.

It was all kind of nutsy, Orrison decided – and changed himself suddenly into a guide.

'From here you get a good candid focus on Rockefeller Centre,' he pointed out with spirit '– and the Chrysler Building and the Armistead Building, the daddy of all the new ones.'

'The Armistead Building,' Trimble rubber-necked obediently. 'Yes – I designed it.'

Orrison shook his head cheerfully – he was used to going out with all kinds of people. But that stuff about having been in the restaurant last May . . .

He paused by the brass entablature in the cornerstone of the building. 'Erected 1928,' it said.

Trimble nodded.

'But I was taken drunk that year – every-which-way drunk. So I never saw it before now.'

'Oh.' Orrison hesitated. 'Like to go in now?'

'I've been in it – lots of times. But I've never seen it. And now it isn't what I want to see. I wouldn't ever be able to see it now. I simply want to see how people walk and what their clothes and shoes and hats are made of. And their eyes and hands. Would you mind shaking hands with me?'

'Not at all, sir.'

'Thanks. Thanks. That's very kind. I suppose it looks strange – but people will think we're saying good-bye. I'm going to walk up the avenue for a while, so we *will* say good-bye. Tell your office I'll be in at four.'

Orrison looked after him when he started out, half expecting him to turn into a bar. But there was nothing about him that suggested or ever had suggested drink.

'Jesus!' he said to himself. 'Drunk for ten years.'

He felt suddenly of the texture of his own coat and then he reached out and pressed his thumb against the granite of the building by his side.

READ MORE IN PENGUIN

In every corner of the world, on every subject under the sun, Penguin represents quality and variety – the very best in publishing today.

For complete information about books available from Penguin – including Puffins, Penguin Classics and Arkana – and how to order them, write to us at the appropriate address below. Please note that for copyright reasons the selection of books varies from country to country.

In the United Kingdom: Please write to *Dept. JC, Penguin Books Ltd, FREEPOST, West Drayton, Middlesex UB7 0BR*

If you have any difficulty in obtaining a title, please send your order with the correct money, plus ten per cent for postage and packaging, to *PO Box No. 11, West Drayton, Middlesex UB7 0BR*

In the United States: Please write to *Penguin USA Inc., 375 Hudson Street, New York, NY 10014*

In Canada: Please write to *Penguin Books Canada Ltd, 10 Alcorn Avenue, Suite 300, Toronto, Ontario M4V 3B2*

In Australia: Please write to *Penguin Books Australia Ltd, 487 Maroondah Highway, Ringwood, Victoria 3134*

In New Zealand: Please write to *Penguin Books (NZ) Ltd, 182–190 Wairau Road, Private Bag, Takapuna, Auckland 9*

In India: Please write to *Penguin Books India Pvt Ltd, 706 Eros Apartments, 56 Nehru Place, New Delhi 110 019*

In the Netherlands: Please write to *Penguin Books Netherlands B.V., Keizersgracht 231 NL–1016 DV Amsterdam*

In Germany: Please write to *Penguin Books Deutschland GmbH, Friedrichstrasse 10–12, W–6000 Frankfurt/Main 1*

In Spain: Please write to *Penguin Books S. A., C. San Bernardo 117–6º E–28015 Madrid*

In Italy: Please write to *Penguin Italia s.r.l., Via Felice Casati 20, I–20124 Milano*

In France: Please write to *Penguin France S. A., 17 rue Lejeune, F–31000 Toulouse*

In Japan: Please write to *Penguin Books Japan, Ishikiribashi Building, 2–5–4, Suido, Tokyo 112*

In Greece: Please write to *Penguin Hellas Ltd, Dimocritou 3, GR–106 71 Athens*

In South Africa: Please write to *Longman Penguin Southern Africa (Pty) Ltd, Private Bag X08, Bertsham 2013*

BY THE SAME AUTHOR

Tender is the Night

Fitzgerald's most complete novel: a penetrating indictment of the Twenties.

The Last Tycoon

A cutting study of Hollywood in all the glittering decadence of its heyday, this was Fitzgerald's last work, his poignant farewell to the Great American Dream.

The Great Gatsby

'It has interested and excited me more than any new novel I have seen, either English or American, for a number of years' – T. S. Eliot in a letter to the author, 1925.

This Side of Paradise

Painfully autobiographical, this series of brilliant literary cameos on the adolescence and youth of Amory Blaine was to define the Jazz Age for an entire generation of readers.

Five volumes of short stories:

Volume 1: **The Diamond as Big as the Ritz and other stories**
Volume 2: **The Crack-Up with other pieces and stories**
Volume 3: **The Pat Hobby Stories**
Volume 4: **Bernice Bobs Her Hair and other stories**
Volume 5: **The Lost Decade and other stories**

and

Bits of Paradise

A collection of short pieces by Scott and Zelda Fitzgerald

The Letters of F. Scott Fitzgerald